ALSO BY
CHRIS D'LACEY

CHRIS D'LACEY

UNICORNE FILES
BOOK TWO

ALEXANDER'S ARMY

SCHOLASTIC PRESS

NEW YORK

Library of Congress Cataloging-in-Publication Data Available

ISBN 978-0-545-60880-0

10 9 8 7 6 5 4 3 2 1   15 16 17 18 19

Printed in the U.S.A.   23

First edition, June 2015

Book design by Christopher Stengel

TABLE OF CONTENTS

1 · CROW

"Hey, that crow's in the garden again."

"Where?" I gasped as Josie, my younger sister, swept past me. I jumped up from the kitchen table, almost spilling a bowl of cereal.

"On the gate post," she said with a shrug. "It's not *doing* anything. It's just . . . sitting there."

"Watching," I muttered.

"Yeah . . . right," she said doubtfully. She swept her hair off her shoulder and continued on into the front room.

"Michael, you need to get over this." Mom was crouching down, spilling laundry out of the washing machine. She brought a basket of wet clothes over to the sink. "You've been as jumpy as a newborn frog for days, and stuck inside the house every night this week. I realize this hasn't been an easy time for you, with Freya . . . passing away and everything, but trust me, this is not what she'd have wanted. Staying in, moping, won't ease the pain. You need to face the world without her now. Nothing's going to bring her back."

Oh, no? I took a sharp breath. If only Mom knew what I'd seen in the graveyard when I'd gone to lay a rose on Freya's grave. I pushed aside the blind. "Josie said she saw a crow."

"Yes, I know. I heard her." Mom nudged me aside to get to the drawer where she kept her clothespins. "It's a bird. A member of the natural world. Allowed to visit our garden as often as it likes — as long as it doesn't interfere with my washing. What's the matter? Are you frightened of crows or something?" She threw some pins into the basket and glanced through the window. "I agree they can look a bit menacing, but you've never said anything about them before. Is there something you want to tell me?"

Lots. Too much. I gulped and said nothing.

Mom sighed and shook her head. "Right. That's it. When I've hung up these clothes, I'm taking you out."

"Out? Where?"

"A garden center."

What? Weren't garden centers places where *old* people went?

She saw my look of horror and met it with one of those smug parental grins. "It's either that or I confiscate your keys, strap you to your bike, and lock you out of the house for an hour. Either way, you're getting some sun on your skin. You're starting to look like milk gone sour."

She opened the kitchen door.

"Mom?"

"What?"

"Be careful."

"Oh, for goodness' sake." She was angry now. "Will you stop this nonsense? It's a crow, Michael, not a . . . blood-sucking vampire!"

"It's not — and . . . it could be," I whispered. But by then she was halfway up the lawn, hanging socks on the clothesline.

I opted for the trip to the garden center. I wore a dark hoodie, which made Mom fuss and grumble even more. But I wasn't going to run the risk of being recognized; some of my school friends' parents shopped there.

While Mom and Josie toured the plant displays outside, I hovered in the doorway of the main building, pretending to be interested in a row of shovels. Twice, I was frowned at by a security guard for setting off the automatic sliding doors. When I moved deeper inside and stood by a rack of pruning saws, he followed me and pointed to a sign saying NOT FOR SALE TO MINORS. I pointed to Mom, who had just come in with a shopping cart laden with plants. The guard bounced on his toes and silently moved on.

"Having fun?" Mom quipped. She put a box of slug pellets into her cart.

Slug pellets. Gross. "This place sucks," I said. "It's so boring."

"You won't think that when you're forty and your bedding plants are being eaten away by slimy beasts the size of your thumb. You'll be glad you've got crows in your garden then. They gobble up the little monsters. *Schlup*."

That was it. I couldn't take this anymore. My mind was so full of fears and secrets. I had to unload them, no matter the cost. "Mom," I said, trying to get her attention.

She had pushed the cart forward, into an area laid out with the sort of gifts you bought your auntie for Christmas: candles, silly socks, books of lists. "Mom," I said again, "I want to tell you something."

She looked back briefly. "Tell me in the café. It's right through here."

Stuff the café. I was at my breaking point. "I've got this special power; I can alter my reality. And I'm working for a secret organization called UNI —"

"Hey, grumpy, look at these."

As usual, Mom hadn't heard a thing I'd said. And now Josie was in my face, holding up a small stuffed toy. A life-size bird with a gray-white body and decorative blue wings. "It's a blue jay," she said. "It talks. Listen."

She squeezed the body, setting off a recording inside the bird's breast. It made a series of repetitive squeaks, like air being forced from a plastic cushion, followed by a row of throaty clicks.

"Yeah, great," I said, trying to move her aside.

She stood her ground. "They've got loads more birds on a stand over there." She tilted her head. "Including this one. Pity it doesn't work."

And she held up a "cuddly" crow, saying, in a silly robotic voice, "Hi, I'm Blackie, and I've come to eat your nose. *Caark!*"

"Give me that!" I said, snatching it off her as she used it to "peck" my chest.

She backed away, making a face. "Honestly, you're such a pain these days. I used to actually *like* you once." A small look of hurt touched the corners of her eyes. She turned and ran after Mom.

Leaving me with Blackie the crow.

I stared into its plastic eyes and just wanted to rip its stupid flappy wings off. But curiosity got the better of me and I did as any kid would and squeezed its belly, trying to make it talk.

As I did, a voice behind me said, "You've been avoiding me, Michael."

I whipped around and there she was. Freya Zielinski. Just as alive as she'd been in the graveyard seven days ago, dressed in the same shawl-like wrap, her hair as wild as a nest of springs. Her dark eyes were strangely opaque, staring, as if she'd left all threads of humanity in whatever place she'd chosen to perch.

"You can't be here," I said to her, backing away.

Farther down the building, I heard someone say, "Hey, look at that. A crow's got in." A flutter of wings made me look up briefly. Not one but two crows were perched on a horizontal metal strut that formed a part of the roof assembly.

"Don't mind them, they're just backup," rasped Freya. Her voice alone was enough to give me chills.

"Get away from me. You're dead." I took another pace back.

"You turned me into this," she said in anger. She raised her arms, and the shawl spread out like feathered wings. "I want my life back. Make me *real* again, Michael. I'm sick of feeding on slime." She made a caarking sound and opened her mouth. What remained of a brown slug was stuck to her tongue.

Retching heavily, I stumbled backward into a rotating rack of cards, knocking it against a display of cake pans. The clatter made a nearby woman yelp — and brought the security guard running.

"All right, you. Out." He grabbed the neck of my hoodie, intending to haul me up off the floor.

But over his shoulder I could see the crows descending. I

put an arm across my face as the first bird landed on his back and clamped its beak to the lobe of his ear. It was torn clean through before he knew what was happening. He screamed in agony and let me go, trying in vain to beat off the second bird coming for his face. He crashed sideways into a footwear rack, spilling hiking boots and shoes all over the floor, then fell against a table full of gardening books. Blood was running down his lime-green shirt. The place erupted with frightened voices. One old man grabbed a gardening fork and tried in vain to stab the crows away.

Through the scrimmage, I saw Freya staring at me as if to say *This is just the start.* Then her eyes flicked up and she caught sight of something over my shoulder. She turned into a crow so fast that anyone who'd seen the change would not have believed a girl had been standing there an instant before. She called to the birds and together they flew for an open skylight. All I could see of the security guard's face was a mess of blood, and skin torn back in shreds to the muscle.

"Michael?! Are you okay?"

Mom was right beside me, as shocked as anyone. I guessed Freya must have seen her (or Josie) and fled before one of them recognized her.

"What happened?" gasped Josie. She still had the blue jay in her hand.

"Crows, gone mad," the man with the garden fork jabbered. His weathered hands were shaking, his eyes fixed hard on the skylights above.

"Crows? *Again?*" Mom said.

"It was Freya," I panted, my head spinning with fear, confusion — and guilt.

"Sorry?" said Mom.

"I turned her into a bird," I mumbled.

"What?" said Josie, clutching the blue jay close to her chest.

Mom took a deep breath. "Look at me," she said, repeating it more firmly when I didn't catch her gaze. "*Michael, look at me.*"

I did. I was almost crying.

"Freya is dead," Mom said as if she'd dropped the hammer at an auction sale.

I glanced at Josie. She was chewing a fingernail, as confused by my gibbering as the folks were by the crows.

I looked at Mom again and gave a single nod. What was the point of telling her what I knew about Freya or the UNICORNE organization? How my father, her husband, missing-believed-dead these past three years, had secretly been working for UNICORNE. And how they had recently recruited me, too, allegedly to help them search for Dad. "I'm sorry," I whispered, with a weight that seemed to anchor at the bottom of my soul.

"It's all right," she said, smoothing the hair from my eyes. "We'll fix this. Don't worry. I know what to do."

"But . . . the crows?" said Josie. She picked up the toy one that didn't talk. She was starting to believe me. And it scared her hollow. I could see a chink of fear in her clear blue eyes. Something unworldly had happened here. Something that had caused a bunch of wild birds to attack an innocent human being. Something that had screwed with her brother's mind.

"Come on," Mom said. She pulled me to my feet. Many garden center staff were on the scene now, rebuilding the displays and restoring order. The injured guard had been led to a restroom. As we headed for the checkout lines, I saw the skylights being shut.

At home, Mom made me a cup of tea, gave me a plate of cookies, and sat me on the sofa. I knew something big was going down because cookies, like chocolate, were rationed in our house. Josie had been silent on the journey home, but the moment we got in, she had run upstairs to report the drama to her gang of friends.

Unbeknownst to me, Mom had also made a call.

I was on my fourth cookie when the doorbell rang. Mom invited the caller in. "Thank you so much for coming at such short notice. He's through there."

The door slowly opened and a tall, suited man with perfect cheekbones and pale-gray hair stepped into the room.

"Hello, Michael," he said in a soft voice spiced with a German accent. He stretched out a manicured hand.

I didn't shake it.

Mom rested on the arm of a chair. She looked nervous, guilty for laying this on me. "Dr. K has kindly offered to speak to you," she said. "I want you to tell him what's worrying you — about the crows, and Freya."

Dr. K tilted his head in acknowledgment.

"He's not a doctor; he's an android. Dad made him," I said.

Mom steepled her hands around her nose. "See what I mean? He's been saying things like this for the last few days. I'll be in the room next door when you want me." And she slipped out without another glance.

Leaving me alone with the "kindly" Dr. K, a machine I knew better as Amadeus Klimt, head of the UNICORNE organization.

He sat down in the chair that had been Dad's favorite, crossing his legs and brushing fluff off his trousers. It felt weird having him in the house, this programmed humanoid that had begun his life in the zeros and ones of Dad's computer. That was what bothered me most about Klimt, the fact that Dad had created him, or had had some vital role in it. I shuddered to think that this *thing* was a kind of artificial brother. "I won't talk to you, Klimt."

He drummed his fingers on the arms of the chair, looking around the room, taking everything in. "*Mr.* Klimt," he said. "You work for me, remember?"

"All I have to do is call Mom and show her this." I pushed down my sock.

He threw a glance at my ankle. "And she will see you have a unicorn tattoo. And she will be angry. But do you seriously think your mother will believe that I put it there or that a microchip was inserted in the tissues beneath it so that UNICORNE could trace your whereabouts?"

"What do you want?" I snapped.

"I told you on the last occasion we met that there would be more files for you to investigate. Nothing has changed."

"I don't care about your files. You're full of baloney, *Mr. Klimt*."

"Baloney?" His purple eyes dimmed as he sought a meaning.

"The last time we 'met,' you told me Dad had gone looking for dragons."

"Ah." He raised a finger. "You did not believe me."

Would anyone? Seriously? Just a couple of weeks ago, I'd learned that Dad had been a UNICORNE operative and not the traveling salesman we'd always thought. That had been hard enough to take. But a dragon hunter? That was just *too* weird. "Why are you stringing me along like this? Dragons don't *exist*."

His face relaxed into a smile. "Yet again you disappoint me, Michael. You will be telling me next that it is impossible for a girl to come back from the dead and transform herself into the shape of a crow."

"You know about Freya?"

"Of course I know about Freya. Agent Mulrooney has been watching you. He was at the garden center this morning. He communicated the entire event to me." He picked up a Rubik's cube, admiring it as if it were a beautiful sculpture. "An amusing mathematical toy," he said.

"It was Dad's. He could do it in sixteen seconds."

He nodded. "Your father was a mathematical genius. But the cube is just like any conundrum: Once you understand the rules that govern it, solving the puzzle is simple." His hands flew over it and he set it down, complete. It had taken him a couple of ticks.

"Slow, for an android," I said. "Couldn't Dad design you any quicker than that?"

He smiled again. "The limiting factor is the observable friction between the ratchets, not the speed of calculation required. Otherwise, it would have taken me approximately one third of a second. And, to correct your distracting catalogue of misinformed ideas, your father did not design me. His role went far beyond that."

Really? It wasn't often Klimt let slip what sounded like genuine information. But I labored too long thinking about it and he was already speaking again before I could blurt out a question.

"Was it deliberate, Michael?" He tilted his head sharply. One of the few moves that made him appear more robotic than human.

I was still lost in thought, wondering what contribution, other than programming, Dad could have made to Klimt's construction. For all I distrusted Klimt, there was no denying he was an incredible piece of engineering, light-years beyond any robots I'd seen on TV science programs. It wasn't just the fact that he looked so human; he could *think* like a human. I'd always been aware that Dad was smart, but surely the making of Klimt was a leap beyond our current technology?

"Freya," he said, realigning my focus. "Did you bring her back on purpose? Were you trying to save her?"

Freya, who hadn't been out of my thoughts all week and was right at the cutting edge again now. I looked down at my feet. "No, it just happened."

"She was in your mind when you experienced your last reality shift?"

I groaned and smacked my hands against my forehead. "This is dumb. I don't want to talk about this. Freya *died*. I went to her funeral service. There was a coffin. I put a rose on her grave. Why don't you just tell me I'm going crazy or seeing things? You can't make dead people live again."

"Not in the time line in which they died," he agreed. "But I told you, Michael, the multiverse has infinite possibilities and you have the power to jump across it, just like a freight train switching tracks." He picked up the cube again and randomized the colors. "The limiting factor is your ability to keep control of the shifts; the observable friction is simply your lack of belief in your gift."

"Curse," I snapped. "It's a curse, not a gift. Look what it's done to Freya. She's not a girl anymore; she's a monster."

"We will take care of Freya," he said.

I didn't like the sound of that. "How? In what way?"

"She will not be harmed, but she must be controlled."

"How?" I said again.

He tapped the chair. "We have secure facilities —"

"You're gonna cage her? Hah! Are you crazy?"

"She is dangerous. You witnessed that this morning."

"I don't care. I won't betray her," I growled. "She was my friend once." My closest friend. The only girl apart from Josie I'd ever really liked. And now she scared the wits out of me. "I'm not gonna set her up or lead her to you."

He smiled again. "Trust me, we are capable of tracking down Freya. In the meantime, I want you to investigate another situation. Something rather intriguing has come up, which appears to be connected to Freya's . . . rebirth. Another force is acting on the changes you made to the boundaries of the temporal equilibrium."

I spread my hands. "In English, please."

He reached into his jacket and pulled out what looked like a comic book. "Do you know a store in Holton called The Fourth Enchantment?"

"Yes," I said, though I'd never been there. It was a tiny place off the main mall where you could buy any number of comic books or action figures. A hangout for nerdy types who dug superheroes. I'd read a lot of science fiction books, but *Spider-Man* had never really been my thing.

Klimt leaned forward and handed me the comic. "This has been prominently displayed in the window, ever since Freya . . . changed."

I looked at the cover, and my heart all but stopped. The comic was called *The Amazing Crow Girl*. On the front was a pretty good likeness of Freya. Wild hair. Wings spread. Crows around her, flying. Trapped beneath her feet was a limp human figure.

Me.

Or so I thought, at first. When I looked closer, it could have been anyone in Freya's claws. The hair was like mine, light brown, a little shaggy, but the facial features were fuzzy at best.

I opened the comic. The pages were blank. Same on the back. Nothing. Blank.

"I don't get it."

"Nor I," Klimt replied. "But this was not put there by chance, Michael. Whoever drew this image has either seen Freya or somehow become aware of her presence. I believe it to be a calling card."

"For me?"

"No, for her. The image was posted up where anyone could see it, but it is clearly an invitation for Freya to make contact. The artist wants to know her story. This is the significance of the empty pages."

"No," I said. I could see where this was headed. "Send Mulrooney in. Let him deal with it."

"It was Mulrooney who brought me the comic," he said. "There were several copies in a box on a table outside the store. Like you, he was puzzled by the lack of detail. But when he tried to go into the store to inquire . . . the door appeared to be locked."

"What do you mean, 'appeared'? It either was or it wasn't."

"There was no sign indicating closure," said Klimt, "and Mulrooney had just seen another customer depart. Yet when he pushed the door, it would not open. He claims he heard a click as if a latch had been dropped."

"The owner shut him out?"

"Something shut him out — but there was nothing behind the glass and no sign of anyone serving at the counter. The next day, I sent Chantelle to browse the store. She, too, had a strange experience."

Chantelle. The stunning French girl with amazing eyes who'd first drawn me into UNICORNE's clutches. I kind of missed her, even though she treated me like a little kid. "What happened? Is she okay?"

"She broke a heel on her shoe."

"So? What's weird about that?" It had happened to Mom once in the middle of town. She'd clucked like a hen, but hobbled to the mall and bought a cheap pair of sneakers to get her home. A broken heel would be a serious fashion faux pas for Chantelle, but not enough to stop her looking around a comic store.

And Klimt agreed. "Ordinarily, such a thing would not have inconvenienced an experienced agent, but the manner in which it happened suggests that Chantelle, like Mulrooney, was singled out and stopped." He steepled his fingers and gazed into the open fireplace. I had a sudden déjà vu of Dad doing that and it spooked me even more than the story Klimt was telling. "She claims the break happened with great force, as though something had either chopped through the heel or thrown a rope around it and tugged it off."

"*What?*"

"As a result, she fell. And though she was not aware of striking her head, she became dizzy and briefly passed out. She said it felt as if someone had applied a pad of chloroform across her nose and mouth. When she came around, she was in the street, being attended to by a concerned pedestrian. The store, by then, was closed."

"Is it haunted — the store?"

He raised his gaze slowly. "That is what I want you to find out. If there is a temporal entity present — a ghost," he clarified. "Who better than you to investigate it? You proved on your last mission that you could enter the plane of spiritual detachment and, more importantly, return from it."

Yes, but that ghost had been friendly (to a point). "Why did it stop Chantelle and Mulrooney?"

He picked up a piece of fluff and dropped it. Another habit that reminded me so much of Dad. "We must assume it recognized that they, like you, have gifts outside the spectrum of normal human ability and that it considered them to be some kind of threat. This is a powerful life force, Michael. It will know that you are no ordinary boy."

I shuddered and looked at the comic again. "And what if I refuse?"

"Then Freya's fate will be in our hands and you will always be left wondering about the comic. I hardly need to tell you that time is of the essence."

"I can't," I hissed through teeth so tightly clenched they were threatening to crack. "I'm a kid — or have you forgotten that? I have to go to school — and Mom always makes me do homework till five." Today was Sunday. It would be six days before I could get into town for store opening hours. And I didn't dare pull more truant stuff, like I'd done on my last "mission."

Klimt dusted his trousers and prepared to stand. "Keep the comic as a souvenir. You may call your mother in now."

"But —?" What about the mission?

He raised an eyebrow in the direction of the hall.

Fuddled, and a little frustrated, I stuffed the comic in my schoolbag, then went to the room that had been Dad's study and told Mom we were done.

She stepped into the hall where Klimt was waiting. "Well? How did it go?"

Klimt rested his hand on my shoulder. "Given that Michael was involved in a serious road accident just a few weeks ago, it is not uncommon to expect some residual trauma."

"That sounds serious," said Mom. Her lovely green eyes contracted a little.

"I think not," said Klimt. "I have explained to Michael that the death of someone close can cause extreme emotional reactions, often provoking mild hallucinations and unusual beliefs."

He had?

"I think these . . . visions of Freya are nothing more than that. But just to be sure there are no physical deficiencies, I would like to have him back in the clinic for a day or two, so we can run some checks."

He would?

"Oh, right," Mom said, her voice changing gear. "Well, whatever you think is necessary. I'll make arrangements at work and —"

"No, no," Klimt stalled her. "I will send a car for Michael in the morning. All you need to do is phone his school. He will be safe with us. And, of course, you may visit him in the evening."

"Yes. I see. Well, yes," Mom muttered, now as fuddled as I was. She knuckled my arm. "You okay with this?"

Was Klimt *serious* about the medical checks? I *had* been badly hurt in the crash. My left leg ached even now. Or was it just a ruse to get me out of school and into the comic store? As usual, his agenda was pretty murky.

"Eight o'clock," he said before I could object. "We will provide night clothes." He gave a curt nod and was about to leave when his gaze locked onto something behind Mom.

The door of the study was still half-open. I realized Klimt was staring at a painting on the wall of the alcove, above the desk where Dad used to sit.

"*The Tree of Life*," he muttered, his accent almost slurring a little.

"Oh, yes," said Mom. She fluffed her hair. "Michael's father, Thomas, liked the work of the artist. I'm sure you're aware he shared your name. Gustav Klimt, yes?"

"Yes," said Amadeus Klimt. And something seemed to whir behind his purple eyes. Without another word, he marched out of the house and straight down the drive.

"He left a bit suddenly," said Mom as we watched Klimt

get into a waiting black car. "You don't think we upset him, do you?"

"I don't know," I muttered. It didn't seem possible that Klimt could be rattled. But something in the painting had made him pause, as if the twisting pattern of branches had sent a viral worm into his high-powered software. It was the first time I'd seen a flicker in him of something that might be called an emotion.

The unnerving thing was, it looked like sorrow.

"Mom, is it okay if I go out for a bit?"

"Out?" she said. You could almost hear the rattle of a jailer's keys. She had barely closed the door on Klimt and here I was asking for a burst of freedom.

"Just on my bike."

"Where to?"

"Dunno."

She folded her arms. Never a good sign. "No, you'll have to do better than that."

"Better than what?"

"Better than 'dunno.'" She had her Igor voice on now. Why did parents always turn into the creepy butler whenever they repeated your own words back? She said, "Two hours ago, I was scolding you for hiding in your room all week. Now, suddenly, you want to go out? What's changed?"

"I'm cured," I said. All hail Dr. K, miracle worker.

"Don't get smart, Michael."

I threw out my hands. "Well, what am I s'posed to say? You moan if I stay in and you moan if I don't. Moan, moan,

moan. I'm sick of it." I slumped against the wall, with my hands in my pockets.

"What's going on?" Josie was slowly descending the stairs like an actress fearful of stepping on her dress.

"Your brother's having a tantrum."

"Oh, like, tell me something I *don't* know. What did Dr. K want?"

"I asked him to come and have a chat with Michael."

"And now I've gotta go into the hospital," I ranted. "And have wires stuck in me and —"

"All right, that's enough," Mom snapped, before I could mention the weird octopus creature that had crawled on my face the last time I'd been in the UNICORNE clinic. Right away, I'd almost blown my cover again. Mom had no idea what she was sending me into. *No* idea.

"Hospital?" said Josie. She took the last step with a heavy bump.

"For a checkup," said Mom. "Nothing serious. Dr. K is concerned that Michael hasn't gotten over Freya's death yet."

"He said I had a trauma."

Josie flicked her hair. "Well, he got that right. You're a bigger trauma queen than Lauren Shenton. If he dies, Mom, can I have his room?"

"What? Get lost, you little —"

"MICHAEL!" Mom was totally in my face now.

I turned to the wall again.

"Michael, look at me."

"No."

"*Mich-ael . . . ?*"

I turned. And I looked at her. "All I want to do is go and mess around with Ryan for a bit."

Josie hooted at that. "You wanna mess around with Ryan Garvey? A kid whose nose you splattered all over the senior school lockers? *Pff!* You're right, Mom, he's definitely ill." She waltzed into the front room and closed the door.

I mouthed something after her, which, thankfully, Mom didn't see. "You had a fight with Ryan? What was that about?"

"Nothing."

"It doesn't sound like nothing if you bloodied his nose."

"She's just exaggerating, as usual. I made up with Ryan, anyway. He was here for my birthday, re-mem-bur?" Now it was me with the Igor voice.

She pointed a finger. "Don't push it. You've been a child of mine for long enough now to know that I don't like lip." She let out a sigh that seemed to last about thirteen seconds, one for every year of my life so far. "All right. One hour. Is that enough?"

I shrugged. "I guess."

"Well, is it or isn't it?"

"Yes!"

"Don't shout. I'm just concerned for you, Michael. You've been a real worry this past week." An awkward silence descended. As usual, she was the first to crack. "Oh, come here." She drew me into a hug. "You mustn't be frightened of going back to the clinic." She parted the hair just above my left ear. "Dr. K knows what he's doing."

Oh, yeah. Klimt knew what he was doing, all right. I looked over her shoulder into Dad's room. The solitary raven-like bird that sat on a branch in *The Tree of Life* painting looked right back. *Fly away*, I mouthed at it, and squeezed my eyes shut.

But it was still there, dark and brooding, when I opened my eyes again and Mom let me go.

I pedaled to the coast road. A ten-minute ride. I did think about calling Ryan. Dumb and annoying as Garvey was, he at least made me feel like a normal kid. And that would be no bad thing right now. My fight with him had been over Freya and who was supposed to be "going out" with her. So weird. Me and Ryan fighting over a girl. Back in fifth grade, girls were so far off our radar, they might as well have lived in outer space. So much had changed since Amadeus Klimt walked into my life.

But I didn't call Ryan. I stuck to my plan and went straight to one of the wooden benches that dotted the cliffs looking over the sea. Mom always said we were lucky living so close to the water, where the air was clear and you could breathe — and think. But if she'd known what had happened on these very same cliffs a fortnight ago, what I'd been involved in, what I'd done, she would have had us packed and moved on before I could blink.

I spun my bike into a heap, sat down, and waited. It was a cold afternoon with no promise of sun. The sea stretched out like a sleepy cat, a dark reflection of the gray clouds above. One small fishing boat was chugging toward the southern-most point of Berry Head. A gull circled silently above, then shrieked and took off in the same direction as the fishing boat. A chill wind ripped at my ankles. The crows were coming. I could feel it.

Simultaneously, two of them landed on the backrest on either side of me, flapping gently to keep their balance. They cawed as they eyeballed me.

And then came Freya.

Two hands slid across my eyes. I jumped so hard that I almost kicked a clod of earth out of the ground.

"Guess," she whispered.

Shaking, I said, "I haven't got long. You have to listen to

me. You have to leave, Freya. You have to get away. I've come here to warn you. They might be watching."

"Shush," she went, her voice rattling as if she had a pea in her throat. "This is sweet. This is how it should be. You and me together. Staying close."

"They want to put you in a cage," I said. "Fly away. I can't help you. I'm sorry."

She drew her hands sideways and down, raking the sides of my face with her claws. "You still haven't told me about the geek."

Klimt. She meant Klimt. She'd seen him in the graveyard the first time she'd revealed her crow self to me.

"He's . . . not real," I panted. "My dad helped to make him. But the people he works for —"

She pushed a claw against my neck, denting the skin. Both crows gave an encouraging *caark!*

"Please don't kill me," I whimpered.

"He *is* real," she rasped.

I wanted to shake my head. Not wise. "No, he's a robot."

"He has a conscience. I felt it."

"*When?*"

"In the graveyard."

Klimt, with a conscience? My mind flickered back to that moment in the hall. "No way. He's not like us. He's a machine."

"Us?" she repeated. She leaned over me and breathed out the scent of slugs. But for that claw near my throat, I would have retched. "Am *I* real, Michael?"

"I don't know," I stammered. "Please don't hurt me."

"*Please don't hurt me*," she repeated with a *caark*. Her claw broke through my skin. "This world, this disgusting . . . existence you've given me, it's like being in the closet with the monsters at night. I sense things you wouldn't believe. I see darkness everywhere. I see it in you. I know what you did to make me like this."

"Please, Freya." I wriggled my feet. "I didn't mean to turn you into a crow."

"Yet you haven't tried to turn me *back*," she rasped. "And you've been avoiding me. Bad, bad friend."

"No. I want to help you, I promise. I just don't understand how my power works, not fully."

"Then I'll tell you," she hissed, making the cut I knew had been coming. "I'll tell you exactly how this *works*. You talk to geek man. You tell him you want to free me from this." She leaned forward and whispered. "Do it soon, Michael. Unless you want to be a slug eater, too?"

"What have you done?" I said, feeling my neck. My fingers were streaked with fresh, warm blood.

Freya spread her wings and gave a grating cry, exciting

both crows, who opened their throats and screamed for a kill. At the same time a voice said, "Michael, roll away."

Instead, I turned to see Chantelle, clasping what looked like a phaser out of *Star Trek*. "Au revoir, crow girl," she said, and fired.

So much can happen in an instant of time. Two weeks ago, on this very cliff, I'd looked down the barrel of a different kind of weapon, a speeding black car. Back then, my senses had responded quicker than light and I'd jumped the tracks of the multiverse. I'd survived and changed my reality, reinventing the lives of the people around me, including Freya, including Chantelle. Had I known Chantelle would fire that device, maybe my "gift" would have kicked in again. Then maybe the beam that streaked out and lit Freya in a halo of blue would have slowed or missed its target completely.

But I didn't expect Chantelle to fire.

And Freya was dead before I could move.

There was no bang. Just *Zap! Zap! Zap!* One beam for Freya. One for each of the guardian crows.

Freya tumbled over the bench, transforming into a crow as she dropped. I screamed and squirmed sideways as she bounced off my thigh. She thudded to the ground beside me, stretching one wing to half its span. The two crows with her were reduced to a pair of exploding feather pillows.

"What have you done?!" I screamed at Chantelle.

She clicked a switch and tucked the device into her waistband, pulling down her jacket to hide it. "Klimt's orders."

"NO!" I yelled. I scrambled over the bench and threw myself at her.

She quickly grabbed my arms and pinned me to the ground, one arm stretched like Freya's wing, helpless. "Don't make me hurt you," she said.

Like she wasn't already? "Klimt said he was going to *capture* her! He said he was going to — agh! My arm."

It felt as weak as a twig in her grip.

"She was threatening you. My orders were to act as I saw fit. I saw fit to use the ray. Now, are you going to be a good boy or do I have to dislocate your shoulder?"

I gritted my teeth and nodded.

She let me go and stood up, looking around for witnesses. "I was not expecting her to transform into a crow, but that is good. Easier to move her. Now you need to get back on your bike and —"

As she turned to me again, I struck her face. A slap, not a punch, but it must have hurt.

She took a standing count and didn't even yelp.

"That's for not giving her a chance," I said. I was almost in tears. "Next time I meet Klimt, I'll deal with him as *I* see fit."

"You are a fool," she said, the blood rising up to color her cheek. "And if you ever strike me again, it will take more than UNICORNE to stop me from putting you down. Pick up your bike. Go home. I need to clear this mess."

"No."

"*Pardon?*" she said. The French pronunciation.

"I'm taking Freya back to her grave where she belongs. You'll have to dislocate both my shoulders to stop me."

She muttered something under her breath. I thought for one moment she was going to zap me, too. Maybe that would have been a fitting way to die, me and Freya in a murder of crows on an isolated cliff top. Instead, she checked her watch, which seemed a slightly odd thing to do, then said, "All right. She is yours. But go now and do not waste time. I will tell Klimt she died like the other crows." She picked up my bike for me. "Go." And as I got on, she drifted back toward the road, where her bright red Vespa scooter was waiting.

It was an awkward ride to the graveyard. Tears filmed my eyes and blurred the road ahead. Thankfully, I hardly saw another soul. It would have been awkward trying to explain why I had a dead crow stuffed inside my jacket and blood trickling from a cut to my neck.

I found her grave as I had the week before. No headstone. One small wooden cross. *Freya Ann Zielinski.* The soil was dried and crusted over, covered with flowers dead in their cellophane. One or two weeds were poking through the cracks. Using a stone, I raked the grave out until I'd scooped a hollow big enough to take a crow. Then I put her in the hole, spread the soil back and patted it into place. I laid a stone on top and the best of the flowers on top of the stone. Still on my knees, I mumbled a prayer. Something to do with souls departed.

It started to rain as I cycled home. Thunderclouds were rumbling overhead by the time I parked my bike in the garage and flipped up my collar to hide the cut on my neck.

"Just in time," Mom said as I came into the kitchen. She handed me a towel to dry my hair. "Your eyes are red. Is everything okay? You look like you've been crying."

"It's just the rain," I mumbled.

She grabbed my arm and made me look at her. "Mich-ael? Tell me the truth."

I sighed and dropped the towel onto a stool. "I went to Freya's grave."

"And found this?"

A black feather had stuck to the weave of my sweater. One small part of Freya that hadn't made it into the ground.

"It was by the grave," I said, taking it from her. "She liked crows. It felt right to have it."

Mom nodded thoughtfully. "Is that what's been spooking you about the crows we've seen, that link to Freya?"

"I guess," I said with a limp shrug.

"Well, maybe you can talk to Dr. K about that?"

"Um," I grunted. Why not indeed? We had a LOT to talk about, me and "Dr. K."

The rain continued to fall. It rattled in the gutters and popped in the drains. By the time I'd dragged myself to bed that night, a vast storm had risen out at sea and a scything gale was battering anything that faced northeast.

I climbed into bed with the feather and the comic book, staring at its cover by the light of the streetlamp in the lane. Now and then, a lightning bolt punched through the rain, and the Amazing Crow Girl flickered in front of me, cruelly alive for a second or two. Who had drawn this? Who could have seen her and known what she was when she'd been so careful to conceal herself? I put the comic on the floor and slid down into bed. Just at that moment, I hated the world and everything in it, particularly Amadeus Klimt.

Some time in the night, I didn't know exactly when, a thunderclap shook the window and woke me. I was on my back, holding tight to the feather. The thunder rumbled again, followed by a shuddering gust of wind strong enough to nudge my window open. We lived in one of Holton's old stone cottages, a place with low ceilings, which had all seemed to shrink as I grew older. It had "original features," according to Mom. Most of those features didn't work in storms. The leaded windows, for instance, and their ancient latches.

The sky flashed blue.

When I was a kid, Dad used to tell me that flashes like those were the engines of alien spaceships firing. He would pull me out of bed and we would stare into the night, hoping for a glimpse of a flying saucer. Nowadays, I never got up. And tonight was no exception. I was burying my head beneath my pillow, when a long, deep *caark!* cut through the night.

The call of the crow.

My blood froze.

Shaking, I got up and went to the window.

In the arc of the streetlight stood a silhouetted figure. A man, slim and tall. He had his head bent low, so I couldn't see his face, his fingers stretched out taut like a scarecrow's. His hair was soaked and parted on one side, clinging tightly to his ears and neck. He was wearing what looked like army boots and a knee-length plain white coat, the sort of thing lab technicians wore. I was looking at a man standing in the rain, wearing the garb of a scientist or doctor. The wind yanked at the window latches. And as the sky broke open a second time, the man slowly raised his head. His lips were thin and tightly drawn, but all I saw of his face was the blue-and-white flash of a lightning bolt dancing in the lenses of his horn-rimmed spectacles. Behind me, I heard the clatter of paper and whipped around to see the pages of the comic book rippling. Out of nowhere, a pencil flew across the room. It crashed against the windowpane and danced on the sill as if spiked by the electrical charge outside. Terrified, I looked again for the man, only to see the streetlight explode in a shower of glass. I cried out and fell away from the window. Everything was now in total darkness.

Breathless with panic, I banged around my desk for a flashlight. By the time I'd gotten the light pointed through the window, the stranger was gone.

I aimed the beam into the room. The comic book was lying in the middle of the floor. I picked it up and shone the torch across it. A diagonal strip had been torn off the cover. In the white space underneath was a clumsy illustration. A wobbly pencil sketch of a figure. A strange little man with no eyes.

A soldier.

It looked like the work of a four-year-old. Or someone drawing with their less-used hand. The body was all wrong and didn't meet with the head. The limbs were simple stick-out lines. What made it look like a soldier was the helmet. I'd seen the style before in a history display at school. A half-round helmet with a short flat rim, shaped like the top half of the planet Saturn. They were worn by British soldiers in World War I. In the drawing, it was sitting on a spherical head that had no mouth or nose — or eyes.

I wanted to call Klimt. I nearly did call Chantelle. I hated her for what she'd done to Freya, but she was my UNICORNE bodyguard and I would have been glad of her protection for once. In the end, I didn't call either of them. For the rest of the night, until dawn broke, I sat on my bed just listening and watching. There were no more crow calls or flying pencils. I fell asleep eventually, waking groggily when Mom rapped on my door at seven a.m.

The car arrived at precisely eight a.m. I'd said next to nothing over breakfast, certainly not about the man I'd seen.

That would be for UNICORNE only. When the moment came to leave, there was the usual fuffle and bluster in the hall. Despite what Klimt had said about my not needing night clothes, Mom had packed me a small bag of toiletries and a change of underwear. "There's some lunch in your bag as well," she said. "Cheese and pickle sandwiches."

"Mom —?"

"And I thought you might want something to read. You know how bored you get in hospitals. Take this. It was your dad's favorite." She thrust a copy of Jules Verne's *Twenty Thousand Leagues under the Sea* into my hand.

"I've read it."

"Well . . . read it again. Oh, and I found this on the mat this morning."

She handed me a sealed white envelope. My name had been scribbled on the front. "Who's that from?"

"How should I know? I don't have laser vision."

(Huh. She could have fooled me sometimes.)

"Looks like Ryan's writing," she said.

In which case it would be something idiotic. I was about to open it when Mom said, "Don't fuss with that now. The car's waiting. Go on. We'll see you tonight. Be good."

I stuffed the envelope deep into my jacket pocket. "Mom?"

"Yes?"

I have a feeling I'm going on a dangerous mission. This might be the last time you'll ever see me didn't really set the tone I was looking for. Yet how many times must Dad have wanted to say that to her? In the end, I mumbled feebly, "I love you, that's all."

"Aww," she cooed, throwing her arms wide. "My baby boy loves me."

"Yeah, bye," I said, stepping out of the house before she could embarrass me with yet another hug.

"Bye!" cried Josie, coming to the step to wave.

Bye, I mouthed, and went out to meet whatever destiny lay before me.

Mulrooney, as he had been in the past, was the driver. "You look tired," he said as he eased the car smoothly onto the road. "What happened to your neck?"

I found his eyes in the rearview mirror. I'd managed to conceal the cut from Mom, but he had seen it in less than a second.

"Cut myself shaving."

That made him laugh.

"It was Freya," I confessed, "before Chantelle zapped her."

His gaze narrowed. "Does it hurt?"

"What, getting zapped?"

He smiled ruefully and checked his mirrors. The car accelerated up the road. After a tense few seconds, he said, "I read the report. Chantelle was just doing her duty, protecting you. I doubt whether I would have acted differently. The cut. Does it hurt?"

I ran my fingers across it. It felt like an irritating nick, nothing more. "It itches a bit."

"Klimt will need to know. The lab will want to see that."

"The lab?" The last time I'd been in the UNICORNE facility, they had taken me to a lab where I'd seen a few white-coated scientists. Could one of them have been the man in the rain?

"We can't take chances," Mulrooney continued. "The cut might be infected."

With slug juice? Great. "*Caark*," I said, not intending to startle him but loud enough to make him punch the brake.

He looked over his shoulder, presumably to make sure I hadn't morphed into a killer crow.

"Sorry."

"Not funny," he replied.

I wanted to say, *Neither is witnessing a cold-blooded killing.* But I didn't want to get on the wrong side of Mulrooney. He had the chin of a boxer and the eyes of a fox; he was the kind of man who wasn't going to break if he walked into a wall. After last night, I needed friends.

We skirted town and drove into the countryside, closer and closer to the disused mine where the UNICORNE facility was hidden. I thought about what Mulrooney had said. Was it possible Freya could have poisoned my blood? Like a vampire passing on the undead curse? Or had she just been making an idle threat? I felt the cut again. Definitely itching. It wouldn't be a bad idea to get it checked.

"Has Klimt briefed you about the comic store?" Mulrooney was speaking again.

I nodded. "He wants me to go there."

"Yeah, well, don't do anything rash. There's something not right about that place."

"What do you think it was that locked you out?"

"I don't know. But it was smart — and quick."

"Klimt told me Chantelle was chloroformed."

"Doubt it," he said with a click of his tongue. "We couldn't find any chemical traces or swollen capillaries in her nose. It was just made to seem that way."

"Would a soldier do that?"

"A chloroform attack? Possibly. Why do you ask?"

"Just wondered. Has Chantelle been in the army?"

That made him laugh. "This is about her defense skills, right?"

I shrugged and looked out the window. I didn't want to be reminded of the ease with which she'd pinned me down;

I'd really asked the question to fill in the gaps. I knew very little of Chantelle's background, much like everyone I'd met in UNICORNE.

"I trained her," Mulrooney said. He pulled back a sleeve and showed me a military tattoo.

Marine. That made sense. "How did you come to be a UNICORNE agent?"

He pulled the sleeve down and drove on a little way, putting on a pair of shades. "I used to do this party trick in the mess. Got me into a heap of trouble." He eased the car into a four-way junction and took a right turn toward Poolhaven. "Sometimes, when things were quiet, I'd stand a row of bullets in line on a table, then knock the first down just by thinking about it, so it took out the rest like a row of dominoes. The guys in my unit thought it was fake. They would say I'd moved the table or someone else had, or I was blowing on the bullet or wafting my hand. You name it, they always found a reason for that bullet to drop — until the day I took out the middle one of nine and rolled it clean away from the rest. That freaked them out. The next thing I knew, someone had reported it to my commanding officer. I was hauled in to explain. I said it was a joke, that I used my knee to tap the table and got lucky if I picked the right bullet to fall. He didn't believe me. Not long after that, Klimt turned up."

"Your commanding officer knew about UNICORNE?"

"I guess."

"So . . . they're a *military* outfit?"

His eyes came up to the mirror again. "Any organization at the cutting edge of human understanding is going to be of interest to the military, Michael, but all you'll ever see is the science and research. I was transferred into a special ops unit. It turned out to be a UNICORNE cell. Now I investigate spooks, just like you. They have a name for us. They call us Talens. Humans with a gift. I move things with my mind. Chantelle glamours people. You flip your reality. Your dad read moods. There are others. Telepaths. Remote viewers. People who can do complex math at the speed of a computer. They've got a pretty good collection of freaks in there."

"Why? What do they want us for?"

His shoulders rose. "No one knows and no one asks. They recruit you, look after you, pay you well, run you through a series of tests now and then —"

"Tests?"

"Lab work. What they call *neural enhancement*. When you're ready, Klimt will take you through it. They send the best of us out to investigate the UFiles — all the weird and wonderful stuff. 'The truth is out there,' as someone once said, but it can be hard to track down — and even harder to believe."

"Truth?"

"The world moves in mysterious ways, Michael, and so does the human mind. Just do your work and try not to think about the reasons why. Being a UNICORNE agent beats getting your head blown off in a war or shoveling fries in a burger joint, right?"

Right. But it struck me that the biggest UFile of all was UNICORNE itself. Someone had to be running it. Someone knew what their agenda was. "Last time I was here, I saw a man in a suit, in the lab, giving orders. Who is he? What does he do?"

"He bites," Mulrooney replied, braking to avoid an oncoming truck. He drove another fifty yards, then turned down a road that looked like a dust track, cordoned off by a set of high gates. "You'll meet him soon enough." He opened a compartment next to his seat, took out a badge, and held it up to the corner of the windshield. A red light blinked on a camera outside and the gates to the UNICORNE facility slid open.

"This is a different entrance," I said as the car descended a concrete ramp into a small underground parking garage. When Mom had driven me home from the clinic, we'd gone out through gardens and redbrick pillars. This was like the service entrance.

"I was told to bring you in this way," he said. He parked and we got out. He guided me toward an old-fashioned elevator, one of those with a grille you slide across the cage, and you can hear the cables straining and smell the ancient grease in the pulleys. Considering this was a secret facility, I wasn't impressed so far.

But that soon changed. The elevator went down one floor and stopped. The side wall slid away, revealing a bean-shaped transport pod lit by a faint blue light. Mulrooney pointed to the only seat.

"What about you?"

"I'll be in the pod behind. Put your bag inside the scanner at the front."

"It's just sandwiches and a pair of underpants."

"Both potentially dangerous," he quipped. "This thing moves fast. You might feel nauseated, but it's no worse than a bumpy subway ride. Get comfortable before the door seal closes. Once it does, you won't be able to move. The pressure in the pod will clamp you in position. Most people prefer to lean back. Don't be afraid. It's perfectly safe. You'll be released when we reach our destination."

"Where are we going?"

He glanced at my book and smiled. "Twenty thousand leagues under the sea. Get in."

I'd always wondered what a bobsled ride would be like. And now I knew. The door seal closed with a comforting beep. The blue light dimmed. Three spots on a console lit up in sequence, and the pod began to move. It gathered speed rapidly, squirting along a narrow tube without ever grinding against the walls. I had no idea what was propelling us. And all I could see of the way ahead was the faint reflection of my anxious face. We were banking and descending, that much I knew, but we could have been going anywhere.

After a stomach-tugging two-minute journey, my body jarred and we began to slow down. The pod came to a halt by a silver platform. The door beeped and opened like a rolltop desk. I grabbed my bag and climbed out. Mom would have been pleased to know that her cheese and pickle sandwiches were still intact.

Mulrooney's pod pulled in behind mine. "Okay?"

Just about. I nodded.

"It gets easier the more you do it." He stepped across the platform to a set of closed doors. He laid his hand on a screen and the doors slid open. Beyond them was what looked like the concourse of a modern subway station, with escalators running in different directions.

"How deep underground are we?"

"We're not underground," he said. "We're underwater."

So he hadn't been lying about the book. "Is this a submarine, then?" We walked into the heart of the concourse. A couple of nerdy types came past us. They were wearing pale orange uniforms with the rearing black unicorn patched onto the arm. They glanced at me but didn't speak.

"Techies from level two," said Mulrooney. "UNICORNE employs a lot of them. They keep mostly to themselves and their computers." He led me onto one of the escalators. "To answer your question. No, it's not a sub — but it is a submerged craft."

Craft. My heart banged against my ribs. Back in my room, I had a notebook that had once belonged to Freya. In it was a drawing of something out at sea. A mysterious craft that I'd never identified and never had the chance to talk to her about. Was I standing in it now, riding an escalator? I looked up at the high-domed ceiling lights arranged to resemble a spiraling shell. How could something as huge as this be submerged in the ocean and not collapse under the pressure of the water? "Is this alien technology?" I asked. A young woman on a stairway going down turned her head.

Mulrooney laughed again. He raised the hand that held the book and flattened it against the middle of my chest. "You read too much. This way."

We were on the next level by now, heading toward a row of circular elevators. Like the pod, each was lit by a faint blue light. "Step inside," said Mulrooney, choosing one for us. "It's voice-activated."

I shuffled in, holding tight to my bag.

The elevator said, *State your endpoint.*

"Level five," Mulrooney answered, stepping in beside me.

The lighting in the car turned green.

Passenger one. Retinal identification required.

"It means you," Mulrooney said. "Look into the camera." He pointed at a small eye above the door. "It's going to scan you. Try not to flinch."

A bright light zapped my eyes, making the back of my head feel warm.

Confirmed, said the elevator. The door swished shut.

"How?" I said. "How does it know me?"

"Klimt, I'm guessing. Last time you were here."

So it wasn't just the tattoo on my ankle. They had retinal images and who knew what else? A flare of light passed down the car's wall. I touched my hand to it, half expecting a shock. "Why aren't we moving?"

"We are," Mulrooney said. "We change floors every time the light pulses. This thing lifts and revolves simultaneously. There's some kind of motion-dampening software built into it — so newbies like you don't throw up everywhere."

The door opened and the car turned blue again.

"This is where we part company, Michael."

The elevator had brought us to a brightly lit corridor, at the end of which was a sturdy wooden door. Carved into the door at about my head height was the rearing unicorn.

"We call this the kennel."

"Why?"

"Because of the Bulldog that lives in there." He gestured at the door. "Think of this as a privilege. Not many get invited to level five." He patted my shoulder to encourage me out. "Remember, he bites. Be polite. Good luck."

With that, the elevator door closed and Mulrooney was gone. At the same time, the wooden door clicked open. I moved down the corridor and spoke through the crack. "Hello?"

"Come in, Michael," said a voice as deep as an orchestra pit. A well-educated voice, what Mom would call old-school English. The voice of the man I'd seen giving orders in the lab. I gripped my bag strap to stop my hand from shaking, remembering a game Dad used to play with me and Josie when we were young. A tag game in which we had to run from one end of the garden to the other without being caught by Dad, "the bulldog." *British bulldog, one, two, three.* That's what he'd say to start the game. I found myself saying it in a whisper now.

British bulldog. One, two, three . . .

I took a deep breath and pushed open the door.

The size of the room took me by surprise. It was rectangular and absurdly long, with a shining marble floor and the kind of decorative ceiling work I'd only ever seen in pictures of stately homes. Three enormous chandeliers filled the space with sparkling light. The Bulldog was sitting behind a large oak table that had dimensions matching the shape of the room. There were no chairs on either side of him and only one opposite him. His head was bent over a folder of notes. He was writing in generous fountain-pen strokes. The backs of his hands were dark with hair, but the hairs of his head were silvery gray, matching the coal-gray fabric of his suit. There was a telephone on the table and an hourglass, weirdly. A green onyx ashtray added a dash of color. Three cigar stubs stood in the tray like chicks in a nest. There were no windows, but on the wall behind him were four huge panels of different colors, each painted with a stylized unicorn head.

"Sit down," he said without looking up. A voice that carried Class A confidence. Someone used to dirty work, sorting things out.

"Why am I here?"

"You're a UNICORNE agent. I control you, Michael."

"I thought Klimt —?"

"Klimt takes orders from me. Everyone takes orders from me."

He raised his head. Now I could see why they called him the Bulldog. He was fat in the face, with flabby jowls of flesh all around his mouth. Deep inside the crumpled layers of his skin were gray eyes shielded by a pair of bushy eyebrows. The corner of his left eye was slightly wet. He dabbed it with a handkerchief while I was looking. He reminded me of a Wild West gunslinger. If this were a cowboy movie, he'd be the one with the pistol hidden underneath the table. It scared me to think that despite his age — sixty, maybe — he'd be quicker on the draw than me.

He lowered his head and went back to his notes. "We need to talk about your loyalty," he said, oiling the words with a touch of spite. "I understand from Klimt that you breached our trust. Spoke out about UNICORNE. That he's had to bring you in."

So that's what this was. A dressing-down. "I was scared, because of what my reality shift did to Freya." I could feel my toes curling into my socks. The Bulldog had taken his first bite out of me.

He continued to scratch away at his notes. Pinned to one corner of the sheet was a photograph. It looked like it might be a school shot of Freya. "Klimt explained the risks when he recruited you. He tells me you were more than keen to join us."

"He confused me. He said he knew about my father."

"You think he misled you?"

I folded my arms. The gravelly authority in his voice made me want to wrap up as tight as I could. My shoulders felt like they'd been winched up by a crane. "Klimt says a lot of things that don't make sense."

He opened a drawer and took out an ink pad and a rubber stamp. Despite the futuristic surroundings, some things, it seemed, could not be improved upon. "Look around you, Michael. What do you see? This is not an amateur organization that passes whispers in smoke-filled alleyways."

"What are you, then?"

He funneled a breath through his bulbous nose. I gulped, thinking I'd overstepped the mark. But no reprimand came. Instead, he reached forward and upturned the hourglass. Orange-colored sand began to drain through the neck. "You're not the first to want answers," he said. "Your father was particularly inquisitive. Ask what you like while the sand is falling. But bear in mind what you already know: UNICORNE is a clandestine body. By its nature, some things cannot be revealed. When the timer is done, we will test your loyalty."

"How? What are you going to do?" I looked over both shoulders, wary that someone might be approaching with a loaded syringe — or worse. At the far end of the room was another door. Maybe, if I needed to, I could escape via that.

"The timer runs for exactly three minutes."

And we had to be twenty seconds in already. Dry-mouthed, I asked, "Is it true about Dad? Really true?"

He sat back in his chair, a look of disappointment weary-ing his eyes. He dabbed at the wet one again. "Your father went to New Mexico to investigate claims of a discovery of dragon DNA, yes."

"Even though dragons don't exist?"

"Nor do ghosts, in most people's minds. Yet you have con-vincingly demonstrated otherwise." He laced his fingers the way Klimt often did. "You're wasting sand, Michael. Klimt has told you what we know. For all intents and purposes, Thomas disappeared three years ago. If we train you to con-trol your shifts, we might have a means of locating him, though nothing, of course, is certain." He opened the box containing the ink pad. "I hear you're competent in the art of flecking. If you don't believe me, read my eyes."

I was ahead of him there. One thing I'd inherited from Dad was the ability to detect when people were lying by seeing minute changes of color in their eyes. Gold flecks were a positive sign; green or red usually meant they were hiding something. So far, the Bulldog had told the truth. All gold.

"What does UNICORNE do? And I don't mean ghost hunts and other stuff. What's your real purpose? Why do you recruit Talens like me and Mulrooney?"

He drew back his jacket cuff and picked up the stamp. Silently, he pressed the mold into the ink. Sand fell. Valuable seconds ticked by. No reply was coming. Wrong line of questioning.

I sighed and tried again. "This thing. This craft. Where did it come from?"

More silence. He lifted the stamp.

"Can it fly?"

"Underwater?" He licked his thumb and lifted a corner of the notes.

"You know what I mean. Can it move?"

"Yes."

I chewed my lip. "Was it on the surface the night that Rafferty Nolan died?"

Rafferty Nolan was a girl I'd investigated previously. Just before she'd died in a tragic accident, she had seen what appeared to be a craft off the coast of Berry Head, the same craft Freya had drawn in her notebook. This craft, I was guessing.

The Bulldog looked me dead in the eye. "People see many strange things at sea."

Evasive. Again. But still flecking gold. I changed my approach. "Last time I was here, you were doing an experiment, trying to get me to contact Dad's . . . consciousness or something. I was in a pod of fluid. Why didn't I drown?"

This time, he gave a reasonable answer. "If you could cast your mind back to the earliest days of your birth, you would know that you spent many weeks immersed in a sac of fluid, not unlike what you experienced in the pod. You were suspended in a mixture of electrolytes and other vital substances designed to aid neural transference."

"Neural what?"

He looked at the timer as if to say, *How long have you got?*

Not long. The sand was diminishing fast. "There were creatures, like small octopuses, swimming in the fluid. Klimt knows I saw them. You can't deny it."

"Is this a question or an observation, Michael?"

"A question. Stop stalling."

He looked at me harshly. "Impertinence will only cost you time. Your father was an expert in knowing what to ask and when to ask it. That is one characteristic you have sadly not inherited from him." He lifted the top two sheets of paper, stamped the third, and let the second fall back. "The creatures are called Mleptra."

"Are they alien?"

His hand went back to the pad.

I said more urgently, "They were repairing Klimt. I saw wires in his head. I know I didn't imagine it. He's not human, is he?"

He stamped the second sheet. "Klimt is a masterpiece of engineering. He is built, primarily, from a substance called graphene, a compound with many remarkable properties, including the ability to conduct electricity at speeds far in excess of any silicon-based product. Klimt's mode of calculation is beyond the scope of common understanding. He is unlike anything on this planet. Comparing his mind to ours would be like comparing Einstein's to a gnat's. He is more than human."

"That's not possible."

He glanced at the timer again. Almost done.

"You can't give a machine feelings," I argued. And yet I'd seen it in the hallway at home when Klimt had glanced at *The Tree of Life* painting. How had they made him register sorrow? Wasn't that what made us different from androids? We had emotions; they didn't?

The Bulldog went to the ink pad for a final time.

And there was something else that didn't add up. In the lab, Klimt had also been immersed in a pod of fluid hooked up to mine, communicating with me throughout the experiment. And yet I'd seen the Mleptra repairing him. How could a machine that was smarter than Einstein blow a circuit just by talking to me? How could I "break" a supercomputer? I looked at the timer. The final wedge of sand was about to fall. Too rushed now to know how to phrase the right questions, I put Klimt to the back of my mind and said, "Is that a file on Freya?" I didn't dare lean over the desk, but I was sure it was a photograph of her.

He pressed the stamp to the pad with a little more weight. "You're a talented boy, Michael, but a dangerous one. Your latest reality shift has upset the natural order of things. You've stirred up the pond. The silt of the universe is rising to the surface. UNICORNE will need to set things straight." He stamped the top sheet. This time I saw the result. The standard UNICORNE symbol with a word underneath it: MAUVE.

"Is that why you had her killed — to set things straight?"

He sat back, tapping his thumbs together. The sand had run through the timer.

"I did not have Freya killed. I had her immobilized."

"What?"

He reached to one side of the desk and pressed a button. The red panel to his left divided at its center and slid apart, revealing a tank of amber-colored fluid. Many years ago, Dad had taken the family to SeaWorld, where we'd watched sharks and seals and other marine creatures swimming about behind glass like this. But there were no familiar marine creatures here, just Freya, floating in an upright position, attended by a host of hardworking Mleptra.

"That's impossible," I gasped, not for the first time that day.

The Bulldog leaned down and pressed another button.

A stream of bubbles erupted from Freya's mouth. Her arms jerked from the shoulders to the wrists. Moments later, her eyes blinked open.

Dark brown eyes. Clear eyes.

Human.

Pushing my chair aside, I ran around the table and pressed my hands flat against the wall of the tank. It was slightly warm and not made of glass, more like a thick computer screen or membrane. *Freya*, I mouthed, fogging the surface. "Can she see me?"

"No," said the Bulldog. He screwed the top onto his fountain pen and put it away in his jacket pocket. "The girl is in an artificial state of consciousness, controlled by the Mleptra. They are monitoring her brain activity and other physiological signs. Don't raise your hopes, Michael. She's deeply unstable."

Even as he spoke, I watched Freya grow a set of feathers along one arm. Three Mleptra immediately clamped her head. One, I noticed, changed color near her heart. A whole bunch of them lined up along her arm. Although they resembled an octopus in shape (six tentacles, not eight, I now noticed, and two much smaller "feeler" fingers), they moved more like crabs, sometimes scuttling, most often gliding across the surface of her skin. They reminded me a bit of the toe-nibbling fish that Ryan and I had seen once in town. For a few weeks before it shut down, a store had opened in a corner of the mall, advertising something called fish pedicures. One Saturday morning, we'd stood outside its window, watching people put their feet into tanks full of tiny skin-biting fish. I thought it was gross and was relieved when Ryan got us busted for sticking a pair of fake teeth into his mouth and doing a piranha impression. But the Mleptra weren't chewing Freya's toes. They seemed to be making little pinpricks in her skin with the spikes that protruded from the ends of their tentacles. Whatever they were, these things, they were helping her. The feathers receded.

I sighed in relief.

By now, one of the creatures had swum to meet me, matching its tentacles to my finger shapes. It had a mauve underbelly and tiny pink eyes no bigger than beads. As it mirrored the movements of my fingers, the cut in my neck began to itch. A squiggle of light emerged from a slit between the creature's eyes and ran through the membrane into my palm, producing more of a tickle than a shock. I pulled my hand away. The creature sparkled like a tube of glitter. It made a high-pitched squeak, then kicked its tentacles and floated off to join the others.

I turned to face the Bulldog, a slew of angry questions forming in my head. Despite the Mleptra's healing efforts, I just wanted to punch a hole in the tank and haul Freya out. "How did she survive? I saw Chantelle zap her. I buried the crow. How did she even *get* in here?"

He swiveled his chair and stared at the tank like a modern-day Victor Frankenstein. All he needed was a fluffy white cat and he'd have been the image of the perfect villain. He blinked the eye that was still watering. "The ray stunned her, nothing more. Chantelle and Mulrooney were under orders to isolate Freya and restrain her if an opportunity arose. By taking your bicycle ride to the cliffs, you made it easy for us."

"And after that?"

"After that?" He tilted his head.

I tried to reply but felt suddenly dizzy and had to steady myself against the table edge. "Chantelle followed me to the graveyard, didn't she? She must have dug Freya up. That's so . . . *gross*. Why didn't she just tell me she planned to bring her here?"

"Because you would have challenged it. You had already indicated to Klimt that you would not betray the girl to us. You had also seen her killed — or so you thought. Chantelle could not run the risk that you would alter your reality and compromise her orders if she objected to your wishes. So she used her wits and let you take the body. A risky maneuver that fortunately paid off. Klimt had calculated a recovery window of fifty minutes before Freya came around. Chantelle

guessed, correctly, that you wouldn't hang around the graveyard for long."

So that's why I'd seen her check her watch.

"You're sweating, Michael. Why don't you sit down?"

I shook my head. Under the circumstances, not a smart
thing to do. My brain seemed to be swelling like something
filmed by time-lapse photography. "I still don't get it. I was at
the grave for twenty minutes. Freya was in the ground for
most of that. How come she didn't suffocate?"

"Because she was already dead," said a voice.

Klimt had entered the room. He walked over and picked
up the file. He examined the top sheet, then enclosed the
whole thing inside a thin brown folder. "You are forgetting
the lessons of your last case, Michael. Death is merely another
state of being — another change of track. Humans, like
Freya, who die but do not make the change become tied to
this plane in what we call a transcendental paradox. *Undead* is
the popular term, I believe."

I turned and squinted at the tank again. Freya's eyes had
closed, their lids like the skin of rotting peaches. Her once-
wild hair, though buoyant in the fluid, looked like paper
strips flying off a fan. She was so pale and yellow, more lab
specimen than human girl. She reminded me, horribly, of a
dead frog I'd seen in a jar at school. Mr. Greenway, our biol-
ogy teacher, had described the frog as inert. That's how Freya

looked to me: inert. "Can she die? Properly, I mean?" I rested my hand on the tank again. Mleptra clustered to the point of contact, blinking like a row of fairy lights. They seemed agitated, as if they were arguing among themselves. More and more lights fired into my palm.

"There are procedures," Klimt said, implying it was true.

"How? How can you kill someone if —? Oh . . ." I reeled again.

"Michael?" Klimt had noticed how unsteady I was.

I fell back against the tank, spreading my arms out wide like a cross. The room turned into a wavy dreamscape. Behind me I could hear the Mleptra squeaking, their bodies frantically changing color.

The Bulldog was sitting forward in his chair. He had a hand to his face as if he was fiddling with a contact lens. "Klimt, why are the creatures so active?"

Before Klimt could answer, another figure swept into the room. He was wearing a white laboratory coat and a pair of glasses with dark-brown rims. He was tall and gawky, as thin as a test tube. And though he had no army boots on his feet, and his sandy-colored hair was combed in an old-fashioned wave to one side, my mind became fixed on the wild idea that this was the man I'd seen in the rain.

"Preeve, what's the meaning of this?" growled the Bulldog.

"Sir, the tank," the man jabbered.

"What about it?"

"The Mleptral interface. It's off the scale."

Klimt hurried around the desk and moved me aside. He put his hand on the tank, managing to dent the membrane slightly. His palm turned mauve, radiating ripples of color through the fluid. The Mleptra gathered to him like bees.

Meanwhile, my focus was still on Preeve. With a croak in my voice, I said, "Don't let him near her!" *Near her! Near her!* The urge to repeat the last two words beat like a jungle drum in my head. I pointed at the scientist. His body shape blurred around the edges. My gaze homed in on his face and neck.

Preeve looked baffled. He shied away from me and went to join Klimt.

I heard the android say, "The Mleptra have detected another source of the corvine virus."

"Where?" said Preeve.

"Outside the tank." Klimt swept around, scanning me with his purple eyes.

"Fake!" I rasped. *"Fake! Fake!"* I felt lighter in my bones, as if I could fly. And suddenly I did. A rush of dark energy took me past Klimt. My feet were off the floor as I thumped into Preeve. He screamed as his hair became locked in my fingers. My eyes swiveled painfully, taking in half the room in one glance. In the tank, I saw Freya transform into a crow and dig her beak into one of the Mleptra, splitting it and spilling blue fluid from the gash. I saw the Bulldog rising from his chair. His eyes were different colors. One gray, one green. I had a feeling that might be important, but only Preeve seemed to matter right then. I was opening my mouth to sink my teeth into the welcoming flesh of his scrawny neck when I felt a jolt of pressure in my shoulder and everything went black.

When I woke, I was on my back, firmly strapped to a hospital bed.

Someone was stretching my eyes open and shining a pencil beam of light into them. "He's coming around. Call me if he goes into relapse." The fuzzy image of a bearded man pulled away.

Then Klimt was standing over me, twiddling a black feather in his hands.

"Hello, Michael," he said. "I trust you slept well. I think we need to talk."

"What's happening? Why am I here?" I lugged at the straps but couldn't move anything except my head, hands, and feet. I was in the same small room they'd kept me in after my accident with the car. One window, a nightstand, a TV, a clock. The same picture of a fishing boat on the wall.

"Do not waste energy struggling," Klimt said. "The clamps are made from high-tensile titanium. It would take immense strength to break them."

I struggled with them anyway, till Klimt held me steady. "Why did you fail to inform me that Freya had infected you?"

"I didn't know," I said, trying to shake him off. "I thought she'd just scratched me. Let me *go*." I looked at the clock. It was almost five. Five. I must have been zonked all day. "Mom's going to come and visit any minute. If she sees me like this —"

"Your mother is not coming," he said. "Earlier today, I informed her we had detected a viral inflammation in the lining of your brain, something akin to meningitis. I did not

have to remind her that such conditions can be highly conta-
gious. Naturally, she does not wish to risk your sister catching
it. She sends her regards."

"You *lied* to Mom!"

"And what should I have told her?" he said, his German
accent crisp and sharp. "That you have acquired the capabil-
ity of physically transforming into a bird and might tear your
family apart if the urge to kill should become overwhelming? You are a danger to them now, possibly more than Freya
ever was."

"Liar." I pulled at the straps again.

He reached into his jacket and took out a small tablet
computer. "These are human cells, developing normally." He
showed me a movie of a thin layer of cells stretching and
expanding in a petri dish, the same sort of squidgy shapes I'd
seen under a microscope when Mr. Greenway had swabbed
Ryan Garvey's big mouth and smeared the results all over a
slide. "And this was you four hours ago." He tapped an icon.
A similar movie played. The cell shapes looked identical apart
from a busy cell at the center, which pushed against its neigh-
bor and squeezed inside it. The invaded cell billowed, turned
black, and then ruptured.

I turned my head away from it. "Why should I believe you?"

"Because it would be dangerous not to."

And that was Klimt in a sentence; I never really knew

what was truth and what was fiction. "Am I . . . ?" I hardly dared say it. "Like Freya now?"

"No." He put the tablet away. "Keep still, please."

"Why? What are you —? Hey!"

He pressed my head sideways against the pillow and lifted the tape on a cotton pad stuck to my neck.

"Ow!"

"Good. This is improving. We have sterilized the wound and treated the infection. As far as we can tell, the virus is receding. We will know more tomorrow."

He pressed the pad back and released his grip.

I snapped at him like a foaming dog.

Needless to say, he wasn't impressed. "You are being restrained for your own safety, Michael. Physical exertion will not improve your position."

"That man, the one shining lights in my eyes, who was he?" But it came to me before he could spin me a line. "It was Liam Nolan, wasn't it?"

Liam Nolan had been my father's doctor, something I'd only recently discovered. He had been at the heart of my last mission. For a while, I'd suspected him of being involved in the accident his stepdaughter, Rafferty, had died in. But when Freya had suffered a heart attack, it was Liam Nolan who'd rushed her to the hospital. So I had a lot to thank him for. But to see him here, connected to UNICORNE, was beginning to raise my doubts again. I didn't want to admit it, but 10 percent of my brain still didn't quite trust him.

"Dr. Nolan assists us occasionally," said Klimt.

"He knew Dad, didn't he?"

The purple eyes narrowed. So frustrating. How many times had I wished I could read those artificial irises? "Many people knew your father, Michael."

"How much did Liam know about the missions?"

"That is not your concern."

"Anything to do with Dad is my concern."

He leaned forward, giving off an air of slight menace. "Dr. Nolan assists us in a medical capacity. He does not become involved in UNICORNE protocol. He helped to stabilize you this morning. He is a good doctor. I recommend him."

"Did he treat Freya? I saw her change."

"We have specialists like Preeve who deal with cases like Freya. You were the stimulus for her reversion, by the way. The virus, feeding back to itself. Once you were removed, the Mleptra regained control. Freya is stable but in a critical condition. If she flips again, it may be permanent. Then we would have to terminate her."

I gulped and laid my head to one side.

"Your concern for Freya's welfare is touching, Michael, but we must concentrate now on our plans for you."

"What plans?"

He closed the window blinds a little to shield my eyes from a ray of late sun. "Why did you attack Preeve?"

I blinked at the wall. "I'm thirsty. Can I have a drink of water?"

He went to the cooler and filled a plastic cup. As he returned to the bed, he pressed a button and the straps drew back, freeing me.

"A show of trust," he said. "Sit up if you can."

I was stiff, but I managed it. I took the water and drank it in one gulp.

"Preeve," he reminded me.

"Did I infect him?"

"No. We stopped you just in time. You were attempting to tear out his throat. Why?"

"There was someone outside my house last night. A man in a lab coat. I thought it could have been Preeve."

He took the empty cup and crushed it. "Dedicated UNICORNE operatives do not have a mainland existence. They stay on the craft where they are given whatever comforts they need. Preeve is such a type. Why would you imagine he was at your house?"

So I told him about the man in the rain. The streetlight exploding. The strange drawing in the comic.

Like a magician pulling a rabbit from a hat, he removed the comic from his jacket. He tapped the drawing of the faceless soldier. "You are certain no one else could have drawn this? Josie, perhaps — to tease you?"

I shook my head. "I didn't show her the comic. Why would she draw a soldier, anyway?"

"Why, indeed," he mused. "Why would anyone leave a signature like this?" He put the magazine away. "Very well. We must assume that the entity Chantelle and Mulrooney encountered at the store has some connection to the man you saw and that he knows of, or senses, your involvement with Freya. Did he see you?"

"I don't think so. I was standing back from the window."

"Good. Then we go ahead with your mission."

"What?"

"You have forgotten what you are doing here, Michael. Your loyalty has been brought into question. You were strictly forbidden to speak about UNICORNE — and yet, you did. Fortunately, we have been able to blame your outbursts on the trauma of your accident. But what will fool your mother and Josie will not fool me. This is your last opportunity to prove your worth. If you want to have a chance of locating your father and, hopefully, of saving Freya, you will do as I instruct you and you will do it well. Are we clear?"

I nodded. What choice did I have? This was ten times worse than the principal's office. At school, I'd get detention for breaking the rules; for the same kind of misdemeanors here, I could end up in a sack at the bottom of the ocean. "What do I have to do?"

"Tomorrow, Mulrooney will drive you to the comic store. Look around. Observe. Buy a comic or two. Report anything unusual to Mulrooney or Chantelle."

"That's it?"

"For now."

"Should I ask about the picture of Freya?"

He mused on this for a moment or two. "Take another copy of the comic to the counter. It would be reasonable to ask why there is no story. Find out who drew the cover if you can."

Hah. No pressure, then? Maybe, for fun, on the way to the store, I could learn to swallow fire and tame a runaway lion? "What if he's there, the man in the rain?"

"Leave the store without fuss and report to Chantelle. Do not engage him. That is an order."

"What if the ghost interferes?"

"There is no ghost," he said. "There is a temporal force at work in the store, but not of the haunting kind. Ghosts never travel from their primary location, and they rarely draw pictures."

"Then . . . who did?"

"The man in the rain. He controlled the pencil and drew the soldier."

"How? He was thirty feet away."

He sighed and checked his watch. "Always, you disappoint me, Michael. Have you forgotten the kind of mysteries we investigate? The man has telekinetic abilities. He moved the pencil by the power of thought. He drew the soldier with his mind."

"Okay, I'm going to drop you here." Mulrooney eased the car into a parking slot and killed the engine. The mall was busy for ten on a midweek morning. Three-quarters of the parking lot was already full. "You know where it is," he said, "the store?"

"Through there." I pointed to a diagonal break between the Comfi-Foot Shoe Store and Pets-We-Like. "Where will you be?"

"Around," he said. "Close." He took out his phone and tapped the screen. "Don't get out yet. I need to set the frequency on my Where's Michael? app."

"Your what?"

"Tattoo," he reminded me.

Oh, yeah. The UNICORNE tracking device. Using one foot, I pushed down my sock. There it was, the rearing black unicorn with the *e* in its tail, hiding the microchip under my skin. Pets-We-Like would have been impressed.

A green light blinked on Mulrooney's phone. He plugged in an earpiece. "Okay. You're clear what you have to do?"

"Go in, be interested in comics."

"No random stuff, okay? We don't want a repeat of what happened on the cliffs."

No. Thanks for reminding me of that.

"How's your neck this morning?"

"Fine," I mumbled. The crow "virus" had been neutralized, according to Klimt, the cotton pad replaced by a simple bandage. To make sure nothing drew attention to it, Klimt had also made me wear a scarf borrowed straight out of Chantelle's wardrobe. I couldn't believe I was going on a mission dressed in a French girl's scarf. So embarrassing.

"Okay, we're ready," Mulrooney said. "Remember. Anything weird, you get right out of there."

I nodded silently and opened the door. It was cold in the open. Or maybe it was just the chill in my bones bringing my temperature down five degrees. Welcome to the world of espionage, Michael. I zipped up my jacket and headed for the mall.

The street on which The Fourth Enchantment stood was little more than a service road, filled mainly by paneled doors and loading bays for the bigger mall outlets. There were two other shops, one on either side of the comic store: a bookseller's held together by dust, and a small jeweler's with a grille in its window. It was the sort of street you wouldn't want to walk down unless you needed to mug someone or cut through to the bus depot opposite. A stray dog was urinating against a lamppost. Pigeons were fighting over half a baguette that had fallen out of an overfilled trash can. Water was dripping from a bent gutter. It was a wonder anything survived along here, never mind a business.

There were tables outside the bookshop and the comic store, both bowed with the weight of the boxes they supported and the rutted slope of the cobble surface. I hovered by the books for a moment or two, but they were mostly wrinkled paperbacks and old car manuals, nothing a kid my age would like. As I moved sideways to flick through the first stack of comics, I saw the *Amazing Crow Girl* cover displayed in the window, just as Klimt had described it. There were overlapping posters of many of the regular comic book heroes, but clear space had been given to the *Crow Girl* drawing. Taped across one corner was a strip of paper saying LAST FEW DAYS. I was wondering what "last few days" could mean when a face ballooned in the window. I jumped back as a jam jar thudded against the other side of the glass, trapping a moth inside it. Behind the jar appeared a geeky face. The guy it belonged to spotted me and waved. Seconds later, he was in the street.

"Sorry, man. Didn't mean to scare you." He smiled apologetically and held up the jar. "Moth patrol. Place seems full of them lately." He took a postcard off the end of the jar and set the moth free. "Name's AJ. What's yours?"

"M-Michael," I said, unsure if I should have used my real name or not. I flashed a glance at him as he looked along the street. He was wearing red chinos and a short-sleeved Hawaiian shirt. Lank hair, uncombed, slightly spotty skin. Aged around twenty-five, I guessed. He was tall and lean, the same body shape as the man in the rain, but in no way menacing. The scariest thing about him was his yellow bow tie, flopping halfheartedly at his neck. On his feet were a pair of creased old sneakers, their laces undone.

He looked my way, turning a wad of gum on his tongue. "You like comics, right?"

I nodded weakly.

"Neat. Come on in. Take a look around. We got all the comics you want in here."

And he scratched his head and dipped back inside, leaving the shop door open for me.

It was a place of bare floorboards and flaking paint, about the size of a large bedroom. Some natural light was limping through a window near the sales counter, but most of the interior was lit by a single unshaded bulb hanging from a charred and dirty cord. Nearly every flat space, including the ceiling, was claimed by a poster of a comic book character. Spider-Man, firing webs from his palm. Thor, crushing a mountain with his hammer. On the wall behind the counter was a life-size cutout of a being called Galactus, plated in armor, with shining neon eyes. I could see now why people were so into this. Crossing AJ's threshold was like stepping out of Doctor Who's TARDIS into any number of foreign worlds.

The comics themselves were stacked in wooden boxes around three sides of the room. Most of them appeared to be secondhand. Some were bagged in plastic and had stickers on them saying COLLECTIBLE; they were more expensive than the others. Despite the dingy atmosphere, the colors were amazing. It looked as if a stained-glass window had shattered and rearranged its fragments in the muscular guises of masked superheroes and villainous automatons. All a bit overwhelming at first. But that, I guessed, was part of the appeal.

"Who's your favorite?" AJ was beside me suddenly, nodding at the comic I'd lifted from a box. The Fantastic Four — about to save the world from the threat of Doctor Doom.

"I . . ."

"You okay, feller? You seem a little jumpy."

"I . . ."

"Wait. I get it. Kid like you should be in school, right?"

I nodded, making myself look guilty. It wasn't hard, and it helped to hide my real anxiety. Mulrooney was right. There was something weird about this place. I'd been here less than a minute and already I was having what Mom would call a feral experience. *Wild animals can always sense danger*, she would say. I was alone in the store with AJ, but I was sure I could feel another presence, behind the posters, watching me.

"No worries," AJ rattled on. "Me and the moths, we ain't gonna tell. And these guys here, they don't say much."

He gestured at a bunch of action figures on a shelf above the boxes, characters from movies like *X-Men* and *Star Wars* along with some ax-wielding warrior women and a couple of snarling dragons. The dragons made me think of Dad. If he were here now, he'd breeze through this assignment. He'd be chatting normally but looking for flecks in AJ's eyes. *The eyes,* I told myself. *Read the eyes.*

"So, the Four." AJ was drifting back toward the counter, his laces trailing across the floor. He scratched his head again, mussing up his hair. Another moth fluttered toward the light. I couldn't tell if it had come from the hair or not.

"I don't know," I said. "Torch, maybe?" Fortunately, I knew the characters. Ryan was a fan of comic books and was often droning on about stuff he'd swapped or comics he'd read. He liked the Fantastic Four. Lauren Shenton had once told him he was uglier than the hulk-like monster the Thing. To her bewilderment, Ryan had been quite flattered.

"Good choice," said AJ. He raised a finger. "But not as good as the man himself, Mister REED RICHARDS!" He lifted his chest and shoulders, trying to stretch like Mister Fantastic.

"To stretch like him would be neat," I agreed.

He put a hand to his mouth and pulled a line of gum. "Sure would." He reeled the gum in with a smack of his lips. "Those guys, though, had their day, don't ya think?" He picked up a paper clip, flexing the loops like a magician caressing a pack of cards. I noticed more clips on the countertop. Every one was bent out of shape. He said, "I like to see new characters coming through, don't you?"

I dropped the Fantastic Four into their box. "Like . . . Crow Girl?" I said. I turned and looked for his eyes, but the light was too bad for me to see any flecks.

He tapped the paper clip on the counter. "You picked up a copy, right?"

Drat. I'd forgotten to look on the table outside. "Um —"

"Aw, man. Are we out of those *again*?" He marched to the door and almost jumped into the street. He came back a moment later, waving the comic. He pressed it against my chest. "Last one."

"Thanks." I gulped and flipped it open. It was just like the copy Klimt had given me. A great cover drawing, blank inside.

"You like the artwork, yeah?"

"Yeah, it's cool. But . . . why is there no story?"

Now, for the first time, his mood began to change. He stared through me briefly, his eyes as creepy as a ventriloquist's dummy. The few flecks I could see were scarily still. He picked at one end of the paper clip. I thought I heard a creak from the room above and looked up to see the light cord swinging. "W-who's up there?"

"Hey, you're hurt," he said.

"Sorry?" I threw him a puzzled look.

He ran a finger down the side of his neck. Oh, heck, the

wound. He must have seen the bandage when I put my head back. "Oh, that was just my sister. We were fighting."

He smiled and rolled his gum. Now I didn't need to see flecks in his eyes; I could tell from his expression that he didn't believe me. Upstairs, I heard a sudden *tuk! tuk!* as if someone had stood to attention.

AJ made a gesture with his hand. *Turn the comic over.*

On the back was a competition form that hadn't been on the copy Klimt had shown me. "*You* have to tell the story," said AJ. "You draw it in the book. Best script wins. You do draw, right? Yeah, course you do. Every kid who comes in here draws."

Not me. Josie was the artist in our family. I shook my head. "I can, a bit, but I'm not very good. I like reading. I . . . think I'd better go now." I edged toward the door. Those noises upstairs were seriously weird, but somehow the quiet was even worse.

"Sci-fi?" he prompted before I could turn.

"Yeah," I said tamely.

"Bradbury? Asimov?"

"Um. They're okay."

He pointed the paper clip at me. "You write, don't you?"

I didn't want to be kept here. I didn't want to talk. But somehow I couldn't stop myself from nodding. Stories, I was good at. Mr. Hambleton, my English teacher, was always encouraging me to write more down.

"Neat," said AJ. "We can work with that."

"We?"

He pitched his gum around in his mouth, bending the paper clip to ninety degrees. I thought I heard *laughter* in the room above. That really freaked me out. "There's someone up there," I said.

He dropped his lip and popped a bubble of gum. "Oh, that's just . . . Alexander — listening to the radio, maybe."

And right on cue, I heard the faint crackle of a radio broadcast. But why now? Why not all the time I'd been in the store? "Alexander?"

His keen eyes narrowed a fraction, as if he half expected me to recognize the name. "Me and him, we . . . run this joint. Alexander did the *Crow Girl* artwork. The competition, all his idea. I guess you'd say he's the smart one of the unit. He likes to call himself the Bof —" He paused and chewed some gum. "The brains. He calls himself the brains."

Alexander. I raised my eyes to the ceiling. The Green Lantern peered back. He had a hand outstretched as if to warn me, *Don't go here, Michael. Run while you can.* But I needed to know about the soldier drawing — and the connection to Freya. "How did he think her up? The Crow Girl?"

AJ smiled and clicked his tongue. "Oh, Alexander, he's . . . totally switched on. Freaks me out with the stuff he draws, the things he . . . senses. You really want to see his inspiration for *Crow Girl*?"

I nodded.

"Cool. Go up and ask." He nodded toward a dimly lit stairway, almost hidden in the corner shadows. "He'd be very interested to meet you, Michael."

Another moth zigzagged between us. AJ's eyes followed it briefly. The ceiling creaked. The light cord swung. I realized my breathing had jumped up a notch. My mind went back to what Klimt had said. *Don't engage the man in the rain.* It had to be him. Up the stairs. Alexander. The man who moved pencils with the power of his mind. AJ had stopped himself saying the word *boffin*, and boffins wore lab coats, didn't they?

I shook my head. "I don't want to enter the competition."

"No?" He worked the paper clip harder. "Great prize, man. Your own e-comic, produced in-house. Think about it. You can join the ranks." He made a sweeping gesture at the boxes, and as he moved his hand, the door banged shut.

I jumped like a bean in a frying pan, instinctively backing away from the sound but moving a step or two closer to the counter.

AJ said, "*Darn* that wind. Really gotta buy a stop for that door. Hey, almost forgot to show you. You get one of these as well — if you win."

From under the counter he brought out a faceless wooden doll. We had two just like it in the art department at school. Models. Their limbs were jointed so that artists could put them into different poses and practice drawing body shapes. But all I could think of when I saw the doll was that faceless head in a soldier's helmet.

"I've gotta go," I whispered, stumbling away. I was scared now. Really scared.

"Go?" he said quietly, moving the doll's joints. "Hear that, Tommy? Michael wants to go."

He sat the doll on the front of the counter, dangling its skinny legs over the edge. I thought I heard footsteps coming down the stairs. Tiny footsteps. Lots of them.

"Let's talk some more about *Crow Girl*," said AJ.

"No," I said. He was staring again, but differently now, almost with the neon eyes of Galactus, as if some entity were looking right through him.

"We're not done," he said darkly.

But we were.

Before I could reach the door, someone had opened it from the outside. A man. A big man. A man I knew.

"Michael?" he boomed. "Michael Malone? My-y-y god, I *thought* it was you."

Mr. Dartmoor. Our PE teacher. Never in my life did I think I would be grateful to be busted by a teacher, out of school.

"S-sir," I stammered.

"Party's over," he said immediately to AJ. "This boy's playing hooky." He took hold of my collar and yanked me past him. "Out."

I didn't look at AJ or "Tommy" again. But as Mr. Dartmoor turned to leave, I heard a chinking sound and looked down to see paper clips scattered across the floor.

"What the devil?" Mr. Dartmoor exclaimed. "Out!" he said again, thumping my shoulders. I stumbled into the street, but not before I'd seen what he had seen. A large moth, wings stretched, on the frame of the door.

Pinned to it by a twisted paper clip.

"Let me put it this way," Mr. Dartmoor was saying as he marched me back through the center of the mall, "whatever punishment the principal chooses to inflict will be nothing compared to what *I'm* going to levy. If I'm not mistaken, you should have been in gym right now. And it's in gym I will see you — at lunchtime tomorrow."

Oh, joy. Pleased as I was to be clear of the comic store, the grim reality of being rescued by a teacher was beginning to sink in. I could take whatever pain Mr. Dartmoor planned to "levy," but it would be nothing compared to Mom's hurt. For the second time in just a few weeks, I was sure to be suspended for playing truant. And there was nothing UNICORNE could do about it, short of Mulrooney shooting Mr. Dartmoor, putting him into the trunk of his car, and leaving him buried in Poolhaven Woods.

But as usual, I'd underestimated them. We were twenty yards from the parking lot when a young woman with a clipboard swept in front of us, halting Mr. Dartmoor mid-stride.

She had long brunette hair and enormous glasses, and a faintly familiar European accent.

"Good morning, sir," she said breezily. "Could you spare a few moments to answer some questions?"

"No," said Mr. Dartmoor firmly.

He tried to push on. The woman wasn't deterred. "Just a few moments . . . *Dominic,*" she purred.

That stopped him dead. "Dom —? How did you know my name?"

Precisely what I was wondering.

Then she took off her glasses and it all made sense.

"Ms. Perdot?" he gasped.

It was the name Chantelle had used when she'd substituted for a week for my French teacher at school. She smiled and said, "Look into my eyes and listen carefully, Dominic. I need to know if you have spoken to any children from school this morning."

"What? Well, clearly I have! I found this pathetic specimen" (he meant me, of course) "malingering in . . . in . . ."

But by then, she had him. One look from her mesmerizing eyes and he was already forgetting who I was.

He even pointed at me, saying, "This boy . . . here. Mal . . . Mal . . ."

She moved his hand gently back to his side. "That is

correct. You were at the MALL. On some sort of business. At the MALL. Why *were* you here, Dominic?"

"Been to the d-dentist," he muttered.

"Dentist. *Parfaitement.* You had a dental appointment. That is all you can think about, is it not? Your . . . teeth. And you did not see *anyone* from school, of course, because you would not expect any pupils to be here. You have not seen any stray boys, have you, Dominic?"

"Stray . . . ? I . . . ? N-no," he said. He touched his front teeth. By now his "pupils" were like spinning golf balls.

"*Bon,*" said Chantelle. "*Merci, monsieur.* That will be all." She smiled and ticked a box on her clipboard.

A hand rested lightly on my shoulder. "Walk on quietly. Don't look around." Agent Mulrooney. He guided me out of the mall, back to the safety of his waiting car.

He took me straight to the UNICORNE facility, into what looked like an operations room. It had an oval conference table at its center and computer stations at every seat. The unicorn symbol was engraved into the backs of all the chairs. There were no panels hiding fluid tanks here, but the wall farthest from the door was filled by a giant holographic screen. Klimt was standing in front of it, bringing images to the foreground or sliding them away simply by moving his hands through the air. I was impressed. I knew most technology could be wirelessly connected, but this was something else.

Mulrooney heard me whistle and said, "It's what we call an interactive matrix. It's constantly updated with a mix of news feeds and Internet links. Keeps us — well, him — in touch with the weird and the wonderful."

"Come here," Klimt said without looking around.

"He means you." Mulrooney pushed me toward him.

I walked to the end of the room, dazzled by the information flashing through Klimt and the rate he seemed to be processing it. The images were coming so fast that I couldn't make any sense of them. Watching a movie with an android must be seconds of fun; it would be over before the first mouthful of popcorn.

He pulled an image to the front and froze it. A blurry picture of a man in a dimly lit alleyway, surrounded by crows. Klimt flicked a finger, and the image ran into a shaky video. The man threw back the lid on a Dumpster and climbed inside to escape the crows, who were flying at him from all sides. One of them got trapped inside the Dumpster with him. For a few horrible moments, there was banging and shouting and the Dumpster rocked from side to side while the crows outside it cawed in triumph or hammered their beaks on the lid. Klimt stopped the clip there.

"Is that *real*?" I gasped.

"Unfortunately, yes. Lately, we have received several reports of scenes like this, in and around Holton, involving crows and other dark birds."

"Lately? You mean . . . since I changed things?" What was it the Bulldog had said? *You've stirred up the pond. The silt of the universe is rising to the surface.* Killer crows everywhere. What had I done?

Klimt moved his hand, and the holograms disappeared. "Perhaps you appreciate now the importance of controlling your reality shifts?"

"Can we stop it? Can we change it back?"

"Theoretically, yes. But for now, your friend in the comic store is a much greater priority. Sit."

I slid into a chair two away from Mulrooney. Chantelle came in, taking the chair opposite mine. She had lost her wig and swapped her disguise for straight blue jeans and a red striped top. She looked beautiful and French and cool. She glanced at me and away again, quickly. Prickly, perhaps, because I still had her scarf. I really wanted to like Chantelle. She'd been kind to me after my last mission. But she was the reason Freya was here and why my shoulder still ached from yesterday. Pretty she might be, but harsh, too.

"So, what can you tell us?" said Klimt.

I ran through what had happened at the store, about the competition and the prize it offered, the dead moth skewered to the door frame by a paper clip, how there was definitely someone upstairs.

"Alexander?" Klimt repeated when I mentioned the name. He was standing at the head of the table, studying the comic AJ had given me. "You're quite sure that is the name he gave?"

"Yes," I said a little hesitantly. Was it me or had Klimt's interest sharpened? "It was weird the way he said it, like he was testing me to see if I recognized it."

The agents exchanged uninterested shrugs, but Klimt, I noticed, had dipped his gaze into the middle distance. That artificial brain of his was definitely whirring.

"Arrogance," Mulrooney suggested. "People on power trips expect you to acknowledge every last thing about them. Anything else?"

I bit a fingernail, a habit Mom had tried hard to make me break. "It sounded like more than one person was up there, as if there were . . . toys running around or something."

"*Jouets?*" Chantelle said scathingly.

"I heard small feet on the stairs. Oh, and the radio came on — but only after AJ mentioned it."

Mulrooney tapped the table. "We need to get in there," he said to Klimt. "We ought to get a look at this Alexander guy."

"How?" I said. "He's kept both of you away from the store already."

Mulrooney shrugged. "Yeah, but there are ways we can —"

"I agree," Klimt interjected. "We need to know more. But a forced entry would not be wise. Michael is still our best mode of contact."

I had a feeling he was going to say that.

He paused as if an alarm had sounded, then opened his jacket and removed a small vial of blue-colored fluid from an inner pocket. I'd seen him sipping this stuff in the back of one of their limousines. It had a methylated smell and flowed with the same consistency as mercury. *Viscous*, Mr. Boland, my chemistry teacher, would call it. A viscous blue fluid. I had no idea why Klimt was drinking it, and it didn't seem appropriate to ask. For all I knew, he was having a robot tea break, though the fluid didn't look like a source of refreshment. He drank the whole vial and put it back. Chantelle and Mulrooney paid it no heed.

Klimt continued, "The intervention by Michael's teacher was fortunate. It provided a genuine means of withdrawal at a moment when Michael was coming under threat. The threatening behavior, however, and the fact that Michael was not evicted from the store or prevented from entering suggests AJ is aware that Michael has a strong connection to Freya."

"How?" I cut in. I'd been thinking about this. "Freya's clever. She changes so fast, people don't really see it. How did

AJ . . . Alexander, whoever, even come up with the *Crow Girl* stuff?"

"That is an interesting point," Klimt agreed, "but one we must put aside for now. AJ will be annoyed that you escaped and will try to engage you again, no doubt. I suggest we make it easy for him."

"What are you thinking?" said Mulrooney.

"We give Michael back."

"What?" Had I heard that right? Klimt was planning to send me *back*.

"There is no reason you should not return voluntarily to the store."

"Why?" That was crazy. "Why would I do that?"

He tapped the comic. "I want you to enter the competition."

"But I told AJ I wasn't interested."

"Then you will have a change of heart. It is simply a means to an end, Michael."

Yes, *my* end, thank you very much.

"Why don't we just pull them in?" said Mulrooney. "Save ourselves a lot of hassle. These guys are powerful. We don't know what they're capable of. Dangerous assignment for a kid, Klimt."

"If we bring them in, we learn nothing," he replied. "I believe the director will be particularly keen to explore the . . .

parameters of this case. I hope you are feeling creative, Michael."

No, I was feeling scared. This was going from weird to weirder. "You expect me to write a *Crow Girl* story?"

"I could do it," Mulrooney said, shrugging. "I learned some pretty good yarns in my time in the Marines."

"No," said Klimt. "The story must come from Michael. He has to know it well, in case he is questioned about it at the store."

"And who will illustrate this tale?" said Chantelle.

"Someone with a talent for drawing," Klimt said. "Preeve claims she will be stable by tomorrow morning."

"You mean Freya?" I gasped.

He seemed surprised by my reaction. "Can you think of anyone better?" He slid the entry form across the table. "It says nothing about collaborations, Michael — even with an undead girlfriend."

"Holy cow." Mulrooney whistled. "That's kinda radical."

"*C'est ridicule*," Chantelle said with a snort.

For once, I was with her all the way.

Me, write a comic book story with Freya?

It was more than ridiculous. It was plain nuts.

14 · CAGED

Despite my protests, Klimt would not be swayed. Immediately after the briefing, he took me deeper into the facility, to the lower levels of the craft and to Preeve's laboratory, though it was more an engineering workshop than a place of bubbling flasks. Everywhere I looked, there were pieces of equipment fed by electrodes or curly wires. They had transferred Freya here, holding her in a transparent cube that floated three feet off the floor, suspended by Mleptran gravity filters, Preeve said. He was quick to inform me that the cube could be imploded by a sequence of buttons on a console he alone controlled, an action that would suck the entire contents into what he called a "structured" black hole — from which, of course, there could be no escape. I guessed this was a warning for me, in case I went for his neck again.

Freya was kneeling with her back to us, dressed in a plain white sleeveless robe. Her feet were bare, no sign of claws. Gone were the feathers that had lined her arms. Her crazy black hair was as tangled as ever, sitting on her shoulders like a nest of brambles. I felt so sorry for her. Despite her threats on the cliff, she didn't deserve to be caged like this.

"How is she breathing?" I asked. The cube was filled with mauve-colored gas. As far as I could tell, there were no air holes in the walls.

Preeve said to Klimt, "How much does he know about Mleptran technology?"

"Enough to know it has kept the girl functioning."

And that was as much as he was going to tell me.

"Can I speak to her?"

Preeve allowed himself a dubious smile. "She's not exactly what you'd want in a dinner guest." He tapped a button on his console to activate a speaker. "You have visitors."

Freya didn't move.

"Turn it," said Klimt.

Preeve hit another button. The cube rotated one hundred and eighty degrees. Freya, head down, clutched at her knees. Her pale white arms were red with scratches. She was noticeably shivering.

I stepped forward and touched the side of the cube. It felt smooth, like a newly varnished pebble. The gas darkened at the point of contact as if it recognized that someone was trying to communicate. "Freya," I whispered.

No response.

"She's cold," I said to Preeve.

He peered over his glasses at a data stream on a nearby monitor. "No, her environmental status is excellent. Her physical signs are good."

"Then she's frightened. Does she have to be stuffed in there?"

I looked at them both. Neither gave an answer.

"I want to be alone with her," I said to Klimt.

That brought a grunt of contempt from Preeve. He took off his glasses and polished them on a corner of his lab coat. "If you think I'm leaving you alone with this equip —"

"Michael is right," Klimt said.

Preeve did a double take. He fumbled the glasses back on and pushed a hand through his wavy hair, wrecking his near-impeccable parting. "I'll remind you this is *my* laboratory. You have no authority on this level, Klimt."

"Then I must either immobilize you," said Klimt, "or place you in a closet for the duration of Michael's dialogue. Ten minutes," he said to me. "You know what you have to do."

He turned toward Preeve. The scientist jumped like a frightened rabbit, dislodging one arm of his spectacles. "The director will hear about this," he hissed. And he scuttled out, with Klimt in close attendance.

I turned to the cube. "Freya. You heard them. I don't have long. Talk to me. Please. I can't help you unless you speak."

Slowly, her head came up. Her face was gray, like a limp wet rag, so gaunt you could have hung a hat off her bones. "Hey, boyfriend," she said. Her voice echoed out of a speaker somewhere, not quite in sync with her mouth.

"Hey," I said shakily. I could hardly bear to look into her sad brown eyes.

"You look well."

I swallowed hard. "Thanks."

"Wanna grab a soda and take a walk along the cliffs? We could catch a movie after if you like? What do you say, Michael? Still making paper chains for me? Still writing my name on your beating heart? Still wanna hold my hand?" She extended her hand like a ballerina — then let it drop.

"I never meant for this to happen, I swear."

"But it has," she said, her voice cracking. She guided her hair behind her ears. "Look at me. Goth and then some — 'cept I can't seem to spread my wings anymore. I'm not the crow girl you thought I was."

"They're curing you, Freya."

She lowered her head, shaking it like a slow-moving pendulum. "No, Michael. There is no cure. They're poking me and prodding me and taking what they need. And when they're done, they'll wrap me in a bag and drop me in the trash and no one will ever know. I'm nothing but a rat in Science Geek's maze."

"No. I'm gonna get you out."

"And do what? Invite me home for tea again? I'm dead, Michael. Dead to your mom and my dad and school. Dead to the flowers and the fishes in the sea. Dead to the beautiful world we knew. My name's on a cross. I can't go back. I'm nothing now. You can't even call me human. I'm like a moth flying hopelessly around a light."

"No. I can save you. I can put this right. They're going to train me to control my reality shifts. When I perfect it, I promise I'll make things better than they were."

"Oh, sweet. Make me taller next time, will you? And make me sing like soft falling rain. And hey" — she flipped a hand — "I've always wanted to walk and talk and sleep with the animals. That would be so cool, wouldn't it?"

"I mean it, Freya."

"No, Michael, you don't. They'll train you to do the things *they* want, which won't include a happily-ever-after for me. I'm dead. Accept it. Let me go."

She swung her head sideways, looking distressed. The data stream went crazy for a moment, spewing out line after line of numbers. I heard a dull beep and saw a puff of green gas mix in with the mauve. As soon as Freya breathed it, she calmed again.

I pulled the comic book out of my pocket and pressed the cover flat to the tank.

She stared at the artwork for two or three seconds. It was hard to tell if she was spooked or fascinated. "You can draw. Whoopee. You got my hair wrong."

"Not me. Someone else did this."

Her gaze flicked up to meet mine. "Who? I was careful, even in the garden center. You're the only one who ever saw me with wings."

So I told her about the competition and everything that had happened at The Fourth Enchantment. "There's a lot of weird stuff going on right now, especially with crows. This Alexander guy has tapped into you somehow."

She stared at the drawing again. "That's the dumbest thing I ever heard."

Well, thanks a bunch. That was me, done with the Good Samaritan angle. "All right, stay here and un-die all you want to!" I threw the comic at her. It fluttered to the floor like a stunned bird. "Sit and shiver in your stupid cube! I tried to help you. I tried to make it better. Remember that, next time you're flying around a light!"

I headed for the door.

"Wow," she said quietly.

The softness of her voice pulled me up mid-stride.

"And I thought *I* was the feisty one."

I dropped my shoulders.

"All right," she called before I could walk. "What do you want me to do?"

I paused and filled my lungs with air. "Klimt wants us to enter the competition."

"Us?"

"I write, you draw."

"Then what?"

"Don't know."

"You trust him?"

"Some. I don't have much choice."

"Got a story?"

"Not yet."

She paused to think.

"Okay, I agree — on two conditions."

I turned to face her. "Klimt won't let me make deals with —"

"Two conditions."

I counted to myself, calmly. "All right. Say it."

"I write the story as well as draw it. You've no idea what it's like to be a crow."

That was fair. I nodded. "What's the second condition?"

"I want to be like you, a UNICORNE agent."

"*What?*"

"Can't help you if I'm trapped in a cube."

"You mean . . . ?"

Oh, my sweating armpits, she did. I could see it in her eyes.

"That's right," she said. "I do nothing unless Science Geek lets me out. That's my price for helping you: freedom."

15 · EXCHANGE

In the operations room, we talked about it. First suggestion: a foreign exchange student. That was Chantelle's idea for Freya. If we were going to release her back into the world, she would need a plausible identity and a convincing disguise. Both would be easy enough to arrange.

Not for one member of the team. "Excuse me? Ex-*cuse* me? Have we just landed on Planet Preposterous?!" Preeve was pacing the room, flinging his arms like a white-coated orangutan. He smoothed his hair into place. It immediately flicked right out again. "We can't let her loose on the street! These demands are *ludicrous*, Klimt. The girl is holding us for ransom. Why are you even considering this?"

"Because the logic is sound," the android replied. "Freya is the key to this file. A file that cannot be resolved while she remains imprisoned."

"But we can't contain her outside," Preeve blathered. "She's a ticking *bomb*. She could blow at any moment."

"Then you must see to it that she does not."

"This is madness," Preeve burbled to anyone who would listen. "Even if the girl can be readied for release, I would need to run more tests. I need more time to be sure we can control her."

"Pains me to say it," Mulrooney spoke up, "but I'm on Preeve's side for once. It's bad enough throwing Michael back into the mix, but the girl just ramps up the danger. I'm also with him on the issue of time. Chantelle's idea is interesting, but Michael would need to prime his mother. We can't just send him home with the girl."

"*What?!*" I gasped. "She's coming to MY HOUSE?"

"That is what exchange students do," said Chantelle. "Once released, she will need somewhere to stay. Would you rather she built a nest on the cliffs?"

Klimt turned to her and said, "Can you glamour Michael's mother and sister into accepting Freya right away — as a visiting relative, perhaps?"

I sat up straighter than a troupe of meerkats. "No! You're not gonna mess with Mom or Josie."

"I'm not hearing this," Preeve sang in the background. "La-la-la-la-la!"

"No," Chantelle said in answer to Klimt. "The child would be easy to turn, but the mother is likely to become confused. She would soon begin to resist the effect. It is better that Michael simply persuades her to take part in an exchange scheme."

"Won't work," I said. Everyone looked at me. "Exchange visits happen in the summer, not during school terms. Mom would know right away I was up to something. Anyway, there would have been letters from school. Stuff to sign. It's a terrible idea."

"I might have a better one," Mulrooney said. He dropped his hand to the table, rolling a pencil back and forth under his fingertips. "You say the sister would be easy to manipulate?"

Chantelle nodded.

"Then how about a sleepover?"

"A sleepover? With a *girl*?!" I squeaked. "I can't have Freya in my BEDROOM! Mom would go nuts."

"*Pour l'amour de Dieu*," Chantelle tutted. "He means with Josie, *idiot*."

Mulrooney nodded. "I suggest we let Chantelle glamour Josie into thinking that Freya is her BFF, then have Josie invite Freya to the house. That way, Freya gets a taste of freedom, and Michael has a chance to read the story before we send them to the comic store."

"What do we do with Freya in the daytime?" said Chantelle. "It would be dangerous to let her roam around freely, even under supervision."

"You forget, she is our captive," Klimt replied. "We do not have to submit to all her demands. We will keep her in the complex during the day so that Preeve can monitor her."

"Huh," Preeve grunted from down the room.

"Sounds good," said Mulrooney, rocking back in his chair. "A night at Michael's house can be her reward for toeing the line, plus it's a good opportunity to test her disguise — that might be important at the comic store, too. How easily can you get to Josie?"

Chantelle lifted one shoulder. "There is no reason Ms. Perdot, the popular substitute French teacher, should not pay a visit to the school. There is also the question of how we deliver Freya to Josie, but that should be easy. I can drop Freya into the crowd as the children are leaving school, having already planted a suggestion in Josie's mind to make sure she recognizes her new friend."

"No," I cut in. Time to punch another hole in their logic. "Even if Freya agrees, a sleepover doesn't make sense. Josie and Freya would never be friends. Freya's three years older than Josie."

Chantelle shrugged. "She can be made to look younger. And Michael's sister is tall. They are physically well matched. It will work, Klimt."

"I agree. Set it up," he said.

"No!" I protested, desperate now. "I'm not letting an undead person sleep in my sister's room! It's not . . ."

"Not what?" said Klimt. "What exactly is it 'not,' Michael? Ethical? Real? Remember where you are and what you are.

Look again at the tattoo we placed on your ankle. You are a UNICORNE agent, involved in a mission to tame the supernatural. These men at the comic store are searching for Freya and have identified you as a conduit to her. They have come for you once and they will come again. We must be ready. Chantelle, go to the laboratory with Preeve and do what you need to disguise the girl. Preeve, you have less than forty-eight hours to make Freya stable. Give her medication to carry if necessary."

"You're the ones who need medication," he muttered.

"What do you want me to do?" asked Mulrooney.

Klimt checked his watch. "Put Michael in the car. He's going home."

It was lunchtime when Mulrooney dropped me off at the end of our drive. Mom was waiting anxiously on the steps, already primed, I guessed, by Klimt.

"Oh, sweetheart. How are you *feeling*?" she gushed. She gripped me in a hug that would have pulped a puppy.

"Good," I said, managing to squeeze a minimal shrug out of my heavily clamped shoulders. Even at times like this, it was important for a boy to maintain his teenage credibility.

She stood me at arm's length, examining my face. "Dr. K sounded hugely relieved on the phone."

He was?

"Thank goodness he double-checked the lab results. I'm so glad it was a false alarm. An inflammation of the brain could have been very damaging." She kissed her fingers and tapped my forehead. "You might have forgotten how much I love you."

No. Not possible.

"Mom, it's raining. Can I come in now?"

"*Hhh!*" She gasped and covered her mouth. "I forgot to tell you. I rented your room to a traveling magician."

"*What?*"

She rolled her eyes and stood aside to let me in. "Maybe we should *triple-check* those lab results?"

I went to school that same afternoon. Mom couldn't believe it. To some extent, neither could I. She'd offered me something that was every kid's dream — the run of the house while she was at work. But I didn't want to be on my own right then — just in case Alexander came knocking.

At school, I received little sympathy. Somehow, word had got around that I'd had a brain scan. As I walked into my history class, there were several jibes about my intellect. Ryan, naturally, had to have a pop. "You mean they actually *found* a brain?"

I threw my bag onto my desk. "Good thing it wasn't you. Don't think they're set up for measuring tumbleweed."

Big laughs.

Ryan tried again. "Yeah, well, everyone knows you've got a brain the size of . . ."

We waited in awe as his tumbleweed sorted out what kind of object, smaller than a brain, might reasonably fit within the human skull.

"A tennis ball," he spluttered.

"Well, that's considerably larger than your peanut," said a voice. Mr. Furzeham, our history teacher, swept in.

Brilliant. Even bigger laughs.

"Take your seats, please, ladies and gentlemen. It's story time. We have an hour of gruesome warfare to get through."

I liked history. And Mr. Furzeham. He was the weirdest teacher on the block, small and skeletal, bug-eyed, with holes in one ear for at least three studs. Rumor had it that he played in a heavy metal band and lived in a trailer, eating nothing but soup. He scared kids just by the way he moved. For a man who was not much wider than a broom, he had an enormous stride. Lauren Shenton called him "the puppeteer" because of the way he shaped his hands when he was describing moments from history. He was also the teacher with the wittiest put-downs, as Ryan all too often discovered.

As we found our desks, Ryan whispered, "Anyway, you're way behind."

I thought he meant with lessons, but he opened his bag and flashed me a small stack of cards. They were facedown, so I couldn't see what they were, but it was clear I'd missed some kind of new craze. I wasn't big on collecting or swapping stuff, but I liked to join in when something was happening. If anyone other than Ryan had said it, I might have been jealous. *So?* I mouthed.

These are MEGA, he mouthed right back. He was about to show me when Mr. Furzeham boomed, "If that's what I think it is, Garvey, they had better go away."

Ryan snatched his bag shut. "Just getting a pen, Mr. Furzeham."

"I'm glad to hear it. Make sure you write with the pointy end, won't you?"

"Yessir," Ryan grunted — and actually put the wrong end to his notebook, which caused an explosion of laughter from the neighboring desks.

Mr. Furzeham picked up a remote and aimed it at the ceiling projector. The whiteboard flickered into life. Up came one of those old-fashioned photographs of a handsome man in a military jacket, sporting the biggest mustache I'd ever seen. "Archduke Franz Ferdinand," Mr. Furzeham said. "Crown prince of Hungary, prize-winning racehorse, or goalkeeper with Manchester United? Woe betide anyone who chooses options two or three. Yes, Lauren?"

"Crown prince of Hungary, sir."

"How ever did you guess? Well done."

And off he went on one of his incredible storytelling lessons. During the course of the next forty minutes, we learned that a terrible war had started in Europe after Archduke Ferdinand was shot. Mr. Furzeham showed maps of the countries involved, and pictures of trenches and muddy fields and tanks that looked like old bathtubs. It was horrific. But the images that got to me most were the soldiers. One was of a troop of British men, all wearing the kind of helmet I'd seen on the drawing in AJ's comic. My mouth was already like a dried-out bug when Mr. Furzeham said, "I'm sure one of you would love to tell me what popular name was given to these troops."

Ryan's hand shot up.

I was expecting him to say something dumb, as usual. Instead, he spoke a word that almost turned my bones to dust. "Tommies, sir."

"Well done," said Mr. Furzeham.

Ryan licked his finger and marked my air space. And as Mr. Furzeham bent down to adjust his laptop, Ryan grabbed the opportunity to really show off. He dipped into his bag and pulled out a card.

A plain white card with a thin black line around its border.

In the middle of the card was a simple image.

A faceless soldier.

I collared Ryan the moment the bell rang. "Show me those cards."

He flipped his bag onto his shoulder. "Nah, get your own."

Not good enough, Ryan. I waited for the last kid to leave, then hauled him up against the classroom wall. "Show me."

"Hey! What's your problem?!" He looked toward the door — not to summon help but more to make sure he wouldn't be embarrassed if anyone saw us. He started kicking. "Let me go, you jerk!" Down the corridor, I heard Mr. Dartmoor's voice and let go of Ryan just as Dartmoor sailed past the door. He backed up and looked inside. Teachers: They could sniff out trouble like a pig could find truffles.

"What's going on here?"

"Nothing, sir," we muttered feebly.

And Ryan added, "We were just . . . swapping cards."

"Cards? Again?" Mr. Dartmoor tutted. "Is it me or is the whole school in the grip of this swapping nonsense?" He rested his fists on his hips. He was dressed in a tight white

T-shirt and gray tracksuit bottoms. Most people would have said he was a handsome man, but Mom would have called him obscenely muscular, right down to the hairs on his arms. He eyeballed us from head to toe. "You pair look about as healthy as two fish out of water. Why don't you get outside and do some exercise instead of wasting your time on ridiculous cards? Malone, do I need to speak to you about something?"

"No, sir."

"It's just . . ." He twisted his nose as he sought out a memory. *Please*, I was thinking, *don't remember the mall*, when he bellowed down the corridor, "HIGGINBOTTOM! IF I SEE YOU SPITTING OUT OF A WINDOW AGAIN, I'LL MAKE SURE THE REST OF YOUR BODY FOLLOWS SUIT, YOU DISGUSTING EXCUSE FOR A BOY!" He looked back at me and Ryan. "What was I saying?"

"That we should go outside, sir." Ryan made a move.

Mr. Dartmoor stood aside and wafted us away. "Well, get along, then. I've got a match to start. I can't stand around refereeing your silly twaddle."

Whatever.

We trudged down the corridor shoulder to shoulder, with Mr. Dartmoor a pace or two behind us, bellowing at more unfortunate boys. After what seemed like a small eternity, he exited a door that led to the gym. I immediately turned on Ryan again and bundled him into the shadows beneath the main stairwell.

"What are you *doing?*" He flung out an arm. This time he was ready to fight.

"Look, I'm sorry." I raised my hands to stop him from running (or hitting). "I'm just . . . fed up with missing out on everything. First my accident. Now this stupid brain thing."

"You said it," he sniffed. He straightened his jacket.

"Will you show me the cards?"

A long bell rang.

"We've got English," he said.

"Later, then? Before we go home?"

He sighed and stubbed his toe against the wall. "Just go to the book fair like everyone else."

"Book fair?"

"In the *library?*" he said, drooping his lip. "You know, that place where you practically *live?*" He sighed and brushed past me, knocking my shoulder.

We clumped up the stairs toward the English department.

"Someone came to the book fair, with the cards?"

He yanked a door open, almost splatting a little kid against the wall. "Sort of. They were in the comics."

My veins iced. "Comics?" I held the door open for a teacher to pass.

Ryan turned and walked backward down the corridor. "Someone told you I'd got the best set, didn't they?"

"No. I've never seen them before."

"Yeah, right," he said, and dipped into the classroom.

Almost immediately, Freddie Hancock was on him. "Hey, Ryan, I got a new Dobbs. I only need two more. Swap you Hodges five for that Dobbs nine you showed me?"

Ryan shook his head.

"Aw, come on," Freddie begged.

"Show me," I said to Freddie.

Unlike Ryan, he couldn't wait to produce his collection. "There are ten of each Tommy," he said, shuffling them into uneven groups.

"Tommy?"

"That's what the guy called them — Tommy cards."

He'd been here? At school? AJ had come to the book fair, with comics?

"What did he look like?"

"Who?"

"The guy."

Freddie shrugged. "Some floppy-haired dude in a bow tie. Can't remember. Do you want to see or not?"

He fanned a few out. On the back, they all had the face-less image. But on the other side were names: Dobbs, Clegg,

Grimper, Hodges, with details of their rank and military history. And in the bottom right corner was a small drawing.

"The Dobbs are my best," said Freddie. "I've got eight of them now." He sat on a desk to get closer to me. "Look, when you flick through them in order . . ."

The drawings moved. Dobbs jumped to attention and sloped a rifle against his shoulder. A faceless tin-hatted man with a rifle.

Not to be outdone, Ryan reached into his bag. "Yeah, but they're not as good as these." He flipped through a complete set of Clegg, who knelt and put a radio receiver to his ear. Grimper was even better. He drew the pin from a hand grenade and lobbed it. Hodges appeared to be some kind of medic.

"And you got these out of comics?"

"Yeah," said Freddie as Mr. Hambleton walked in, calling for quiet. "Gonna get some more tonight, aren't we, Ryan?"

"Where from?" I said, thinking they were going to The Fourth Enchantment.

Ryan grimaced as if my brain really had gone soft. "Um, book fair . . . ?" he reminded me.

Of course, the fairs lasted for days.

"Hey, Ryan, you didn't send me a Tommy card, did you?"

"What?"

"Did you push an envelope through my door the day I went into the hospital?" I'd only just remembered it. I felt my inside pocket. Drat. Wrong jacket. Of course. I hadn't gone to UNICORNE in my school uniform.

Ryan screwed up his face. "You're nuts," he said. He flicked through his set of Grimper again.

The faceless soldier lobbed his grenade.

Bang. *You're dead*, he seemed to be saying.

In the library. After school.

Showtime.

Now I had a problem. A serious problem. I'd forgotten to bring my phone into school. There was no way I could warn Chantelle or Mulrooney that AJ might be in the library tonight. And even if I borrowed someone else's cell, I couldn't remember the UNICORNE numbers. That left me two options: chicken out or face AJ in the library with only Freddie and Ryan for backup.

I chose to go. Half the kids in my class had the same idea; I figured I'd be safe in a crowd.

As soon as classes were done, we descended on the book fair like a posse of cowboys, only to meet another group of boys at the bottom of the library stairs.

It was immediately clear that something was wrong. Long-faced boys were drifting past us, ebbing away like melting ice.

"What's happening?" said Freddie. "Where are you going?"

Iain Grant, one of the few kids not carrying a stack of Tommy cards, said, "It's closed."

"Oh, what?" moaned Ryan, dropping his shoulders.

"There's a sign," said Iain. "Mrs. Rowley's ill." Mrs. Rowley was the school librarian, one of my favorite members of the staff.

"So?" said Ryan with a selfish grunt.

"So the book fair's canceled, dimwit."

"But are the comics in there? Is the guy around?"

"How should I know?" said Iain.

Ryan sighed. "I'm gonna look." He pounded up the stairs, two at a time.

"There's no point," said Iain. He stopped me and Freddie from following Ryan. "Door's locked. Lights are off."

Freddie shrugged. He hitched his bag to the opposite shoulder. "I'm going, then. I don't want to be waiting in the rain for a bus. See you, Michael."

"Yeah, see you," I muttered. And he walked away, talking swaps with Iain.

I heard a thud at the top of the stairs and ran up. Ryan was banging his head against the pane of glass in the library door. I saw the closed sign and the unlit interior. A feeling of relief flooded through me.

"Come on, Ryan. There's no point hanging around."

"It's not fair," he said. "I only need three Hodges and a Dobbs and I win."

"Win?" I said. "What do you win?"

"My story in a comic." He pounded the door with his fist. It gave a slight click and moved a notch.

"Awesome!" he shrieked. "Hah! It's open!"

"Ryan, wait."

But there was no stopping him. He put his weight against the door and barged right in.

I had no choice but to follow. "Ryan! Leave it. Come on. We'll get into trouble." More trouble than he knew. I was certain I'd heard the click of the door latch a fraction before his fist had struck. What if AJ — or Alexander — was in here waiting? I fumbled for the panel of light switches that I knew was just inside the door. I had been, at times, a library helper. Turning off the lights had been one of my jobs at the end of our book club. Now, all I could think about was turning them on. I flipped the whole set with a sweep of my hand.

Nothing. The lights were dead.

"Ryan! Get out. It's not safe!" I shouted.

"Don't be such a loser," he said. "Look, there are loads of them!" He was darting back and forth, gathering up cards. The library was a basic rectangular room with shelves built into the longer walls and some carousels of paperbacks between the tables. At the farthest end was a picture window that looked down onto the school's main entrance and a foun-tain we called the yacking fish. (It vomited water from a fish's mouth due to a faulty pump.) I decided to check the circulation desk, where Mrs. Rowley normally sat. It was the only place a man could have hidden. Picking up a hardback dictionary, I took a deep breath and launched myself. Nothing. An empty chair and a wastepaper basket. A stack of returned books on the floor.

"Hey, there's a new one." The tempo of Ryan's search increased. He bounced off the tables and spun a carousel. Then, suddenly, he skidded to a halt.

"What's the matter?" I said, still peering around. The carousels weren't wide enough to hide a man's body and there was nothing under any of the tables. But AJ was here. I could sense it. And now I thought I could hear it, too. The ghostly sound of marching feet.

"Ryan, do you hear that?" I whipped around and looked at the door. It had closed by itself. *"Ryan,"* I hissed. "We've gotta get out of here!"

Ryan was clapping his hands, slowly approaching the only other piece of furniture in the library — a folding book cart.

He flipped two catches and swung the cart open. His eyes lit up as if he'd just entered a pharaoh's tomb. He snatched up a comic. A slim pack of Tommy cards fell to the floor. "Magic," he breathed. He slammed the comic down and picked up the cards. "Yes!" he said in triumph, pulling an invisible chain with his fist.

By then I was on him, tugging his arm. "Come on. I mean it. We've got to run."

He pushed me off and ran to the window, where he could see the new cards better. He ripped the pack open. "These are *cool.*"

A carousel turned. A whole strip of paperbacks clattered to the floor. Ryan, too immersed in his cards, didn't notice it.

One last time, I shouted his name.

Then the cart began to move.

Once it started, it moved like a car burning rubber at a light. As it bore down on Ryan, I screamed his name and my head went through a familiar routine — a slight touch of dizziness, a moment of breathlessness. I squeezed my eyes shut. *Idiot* was all I could think as I tried to picture Ryan anywhere but against that window.

The cart went through it with the force of a two-ton truck. I covered my ears as the window shattered and glass rained down on the courtyard below. I heard a thump and a wrenching of metal. A spray of water flowered past the window. A young girl screamed. Shell-shocked, I staggered to the window and looked down. The cart had landed on top of the fountain, demolishing the fish and the dais the fountain sat on. Water was jetting from a broken pipe, spraying outward, flooding the courtyard. Books and comics were everywhere. Two men and a woman ran out of the school's reception area. One of them was Mr. Solomon, the principal. "Turn off the water!" he shouted to the other man — Eric, the janitor. I stood back from the window as Solomon looked up to see where the cart had come from. And that's when I saw Alexander, a white-coated figure in horn-rimmed glasses and army boots, standing on the flat roof opposite the library. Just like the time in the rain, he had his arms stretched out in a taut umbrella shape. Without looking at the library, he backed away and went down an isolated fire escape into the school parking lot. I saw him take off his glasses and get into a van before calmly driving away.

I looked again at the wreckage. There was no sign of Ryan.

But on the floor where he'd been standing were the cards he'd been looking at before the crash. I picked one up and was almost sick. In the corner where Dobbs and the other men had been was a picture of a scientist in a lab coat and glasses. Diagonally opposite the drawing were his details.

The Boffin.

At school, the fallout was horrendous. The next morning, Mr. Solomon rounded up every boy (and two girls) who were known to have collected Tommy cards or swapped them. All cards were confiscated and use of them in school was strictly prohibited. Anyone seen with them would immediately be suspended, Mr. Solomon told a school assembly. Whoever had committed this appalling act of vandalism would be tracked down and dealt with — and made to pay.

He interviewed all of us, including, at length, me, Freddie, Iain Grant, and a very confused Ryan Garvey.

I'd tried to call Ryan after the incident, only to hear that his phone was off. I spent most of the night fretting that I'd killed him or pasted him into an alternate universe. To my relief, he'd turned up at school as usual, safe and unbruised, but strangely withdrawn.

"You okay?" I'd asked him, expecting the usual arrogant grunt. Instead, he'd shied away and sat alone at a desk, hidden behind a book. Whoa. Call the documentary makers. Ryan Garvey with a book was like the eighth wonder of the world. If anyone approached him, he said he was reading (the ninth wonder of the world!) and flapped them away. Something was definitely wrong. I knew I'd saved his life last night by changing my reality at the crucial moment. But what had it done to him? We'd been in the library, I reminded myself. But Ryan the bookworm? Surely that hadn't been in my head?

I got my answer during my stint in the principal's study.

Mrs. Greaves, his secretary, marched me in. "Shoulders back, hands at your sides." That in itself was pretty unnerving. I half expected to look through the window and see Mr. Tavistock's woodworking class constructing a gallows out in the yard.

Mr. Solomon was sitting at his desk, swiveling his huge leather chair. His gaze never left my face as he spoke. "The people over here are three of the school governors."

I glanced to my right. Two men and a woman were on a row of chairs. One of the men was sitting forward wringing his hands, head bent low. The woman's expression was as dour as the crumpled fish outside.

"Look at me, not at them," Mr. Solomon said. "They are here at my request, to listen and observe. The young lady on your left is Janice Maywater. She is the school relationship counselor. She is here to make sure you have a fair hearing. I'll come straight to the point, Malone. I understand that you were one of the last boys to visit the library after school yesterday?"

"Yes, sir."

"Was anyone with you?"

"Just Ryan, sir."

"Ryan Garvey?"

"Sir."

His eyes flicked down to his desk. Janice Maywater scribbled something on a notepad. One of the governors breathed in sharply.

"Tell us why you went to the library, Michael."

"For the book fair, sir."

"The book fair that was canceled by a notice from Mrs. Rowley, correct?"

I nodded.

"Did you find the library open or locked?"

"Locked, sir."

"Was there anyone in there?"

I shook my head. "The lights were off."

"I see. And Ryan was with you at this time?"

Why was he going on about Ryan? "Yes — sir." I glanced to my right. The governor nearest to me was stirring the air with the toe of his shoe.

"Look at me, Michael."

I found Mr. Solomon's gaze again.

"Did you force the door open?"

"No, sir."

"Are you *sure* about that?"

"Yes, sir. Positive." What, I wondered, had Ryan told him?

"But you tried the door, didn't you?"

I shrugged. "It was locked."

"So you made no attempt to force your way in?"

Janice Maywater raised her hand. The principal gave a tight-lipped nod. She said, "Did anyone with you force the door, Michael? Or anyone after you, perhaps?"

"I don't know, miss." I shook my head. They were starting to confuse me now.

Ms. Maywater threw me a troubled look. "Michael, you do know that if you're found to be lying, the consequences will be very serious?"

"Honest, miss. I didn't break in — and neither did Ryan."

"Well, on the subject of Ryan." Mr. Solomon was swift to take the lead again. "How do you explain this?" He threw a newspaper to the front of the desk. "Go on. Take a look."

I stepped forward and peered at it. On a page of the *Holton Post* was a picture of Ryan sitting in the medieval stocks that were one of Holton's tourist "attractions." Around his neck was a sign saying IDIOT. Nearly every kid in Holton had stuck their head in those stocks at some point, but *idiot* was the last thought in my mind when I'd changed my reality.

Faster than the speed of light, I must have pictured Ryan there and rearranged the time lines to make it happen. Now the emphasis on him began to make sense.

"You look puzzled, Michael." Mr. Solomon steepled his fingers as if his hands were a snare in which he might catch me. He leaned forward and tapped the picture. "Let me clarify something for you. I rang the *Holton Post* this morning. This photograph was taken at around three twenty-five yesterday. So unless you've reinvented the laws of physics and somehow made Mr. Garvey appear in two places at once, he couldn't have been with you at the library, could he?"

"But Freddie and Iain —?"

"Oh, yes, Hancock and Grant have given us the same bit of flimflam. Garvey led the charge to the library. Garvey was the one most deeply disappointed about the cancellation. And therefore, Garvey, a known troublemaker, by implication broke into the library, pushed a cart through a plate-glass window, and caused more than three thousand dollars' worth of damage. But we both know that's not true, don't we? I'm afraid you've been undone, Michael. Your carefully thought-out plan has been derailed by virtue of a timely piece of journalism."

"Mr. Solomon —?" Janice Maywater tried to cut in.

But Solomon was steaming now. He had me in the crosshairs of his sights. "I will ask you plainly and you will answer me true: Did you or did you not go into the library last night and push that book cart through the window?"

I looked down at my feet.

"Answer me, boy!"

"NO, SIR!" I shouted across the table. A tear rolled out of my eye.

The toe-flipping governor slapped his knee. "Then why are you lying about this fool Garvey?"

Mr. Solomon's gaze turned laser sharp. One chance, that was all I had.

"Because . . ." Think of something, Michael. *Think.* "Because he was crowing about having the best cards, sir."

They paused for breath. We *all* paused for breath.

"So you thought you'd implicate your friend? For having a better set of . . . *cards* than you?" Mr. Solomon was incredulous with fury.

"I'm sorry," I said, hanging my head in shame. Shame that I'd had to lie about Ryan. Shame that I couldn't speak the whole truth.

Janice Maywater said, "Mr. Solomon, rightly or wrongly, it's not uncommon for teenage boys to engage in this kind of competitive falsehood."

"Not in my school!" he thundered. He leveled a finger. "I don't believe it. Not for one moment. You're in this up to your neck, Malone. The police have been informed about this incident. If they find your fingerprints on that cart, nothing on this earth will save you from my wrath."

Oh, no? How about the UNICORNE organization? I so wanted to thump his desk and tell him I *had* reinvented the laws of physics. Wisely, I kept my mouth shut.

"Get out," he snapped, swinging his chair toward the governors. "And don't think you've heard the last of this."

I backed away, unsteady on my feet. Janice Maywater began to stand up to help me. She sat down again as the second male governor took my arm and guided me toward the door. "Don't look at me," he whispered. "School gates. Rear entrance. Break time. Be there."

I didn't need to look at him to know who he was. I recognized the gravelly tone in his voice.

It was the UNICORNE director.

The Bulldog.

20 · GAUNTLET

When the bell rang for morning break, I made the excuse that I needed the restroom and escaped from Ryan and the other boys, who were anxious to know how I'd gotten on with Solomon. I cut across the hall and through the kitchens, carefully avoiding the chatting lunch ladies. I hurried across a small delivery yard and into the road. A black car was waiting outside the rear gates, its engine running. One of its doors clicked open. I dipped my head and got in.

The Bulldog was in the backseat. "Drive around the block," he said to Mulrooney, who was behind the wheel as usual.

"I can't stay," I said nervously. "If I'm gone the whole break, the others will look for me. How did you get into Solomon's office?"

The Bulldog stroked the underside of his chin, using his fingers in a razorlike action. A smell of cigarette smoke was clinging to his suit. "I *am* a school governor," he replied. "A degree of normality can be useful in situations such as this. I've brought you here to tell you what's going to happen. By the end of the morning, the governors will have

Josie was. No hint of the moody Goth. "How did you ~~nge~~ her eyes?" I asked. They'd miraculously gone from ~~wn~~ to pale blue.

"Colored contact lenses," Mulrooney said.

A crow in contacts. That was kind of surreal.

The Bulldog wiggled a finger, meaning I should put the ~~apers~~ away. "Read it — in private — and then destroy it. ~~ou~~ need to know what your sister will be primed with and ~~what~~ you have in common with . . . Miss Winters. Tomorrow, ~~after~~ school, she will come to your house. On Friday morn~~ing~~, you will go to the comic store together. A car will come ~~to~~ pick you up at home. Don't be late. Let the boy out now, please."

The car pulled up and the door clicked open. "By the way," the Bulldog said, staring at his fingernails as if they'd been surgically renewed overnight, "the reality shift was most impressive. Have you noticed any consequences, other than Garvey's embarrassing predicament?"

"No. I don't think so."

"Good. You're beginning to perfect the gift. Your father would have been proud of you."

As he said this, we made eye contact for a moment. Though the interior of the car was dark, his eyes appeared to be a uniform color. I blinked for a moment and seemed to recall that during my attack on Preeve, I'd seen one green iris

recommended to the principal that you, Garvey, Hancock, and Grant be suspended for two days, pending an inquiry."

"What?!"

"A carefully worded letter will be sent to your mother. You performed well in there, but Solomon wants a result. Your little gang of friends are his primary suspects. I am not about to disabuse him of that, especially as UNICORNE needs you in the field. Our targets at the comic store have stepped up their intent. They have thrown down a gauntlet, which you will pick up. I want this file resolved, quickly. Now, pay attention. I need to ask you some questions about the incident."

"I told Chantelle everything last night." I'd texted her after I'd run from the library and we'd had a brief conversation at home. Her instructions were to stay put and act as if nothing had happened. So I'd done exactly that, burying my head in homework all evening. Meeting the Bulldog in Solomon's office was the first indication that UNICORNE was actively on the case.

"She says you found new cards. I take it you have them?"

I nodded. I'd sealed the Boffin cards in an envelope and hidden them inside my shirt — a trick Dad had taught me long ago for smuggling birthday cards past Mom.

The Bulldog flipped through them. He stared at the image as if it meant more to him than he wanted to reveal.

"He doesn't do much," I said. Unlike the soldiers, the Boffin figure just stood, head bent, in his lab coat and boots. All that moved were his arms, which lifted slowly from his sides to make the intimidating A shape.

"He doesn't need to do anything," the Bulldog muttered, his cheeks wobbling with every word. "This is simply the image he uses when he commands his men."

"Men?" I said.

"The soldiers on the cards," Mulrooney said. "People with telekinetic ability always use some form of visualization to help them concentrate their mind. We think this Boffin-slash-Alexander guy has created an imaginary troop of soldiers that he uses to carry out sorties for him. The heel of Chantelle's shoe, for instance. He'll picture them laying a rope on the floor, and when she puts her foot in the right position, he'll imagine them pulling the rope against the heel with enough force to break it off the shoe. With practice, I could achieve a task like that. But moving that cart through the window, at speed? That would take a vast amount of con-centration. It's a neat method, you might even say beautiful. I'd admire him if he wasn't so dangerous."

A troop of soldiers? That would explain the ghostly foot-steps. Enough for an army.

Alexander's Army.

I tightened my fists and shuddered.

The Bulldog slipped the cards into h⸻ touch the cart?"

"No, but Ryan did."

"We're onto the cart, sir," Mulrooney s⸻ teams was on the scene right away. All the p⸻ a bunch of smears. Tell me about the van you⸻ get into, Michael."

"It was white, a bit dirty."

"Any lettering?"

"No." I looked at the Bulldog, who was worki⸻ food off his teeth. "What did you mean when you⸻ picking up the gauntlet?"

"You will stay at home tomorrow and memoriz⸻ handed me an unsealed envelope from his lap. "It⸻ details of Freya's new identity."

I lifted the flap and teased out the first page. ⸻ Winters? That's her new name?"

"Her choice," said Mulrooney. "Check out the ⸻ graph."

I pulled the page to halfway. "Wow. That's *Freya*?"

"They've done a good job with her," Mulrooney said.⸻

No, they'd done an *amazing* job. They'd bleached ⸻ eyebrows and given her blond hair down to her shoulde⸻ Her nose stud had been removed and the hole patched u⸻ She looked incredibly young. Innocently pretty, in the sam⸻

and one gray. How could that be? I immediately looked for flecks, but by then he was turning away, saying, "Try to stay out of trouble, Michael."

And they dropped me back where they'd picked me up, and drove away quickly into the rain.

Mom sank onto the sofa in slow, slow motion, the letter from Solomon quivering in her hands. "Please tell me you had nothing to do with this." Her voice was as fragile as a pine needle falling off a Christmas tree.

"You should see the fountain," Josie babbled. "It's like . . . *urk*." She put her head sideways and stuck out her tongue.

"Josie, go upstairs and get changed," said Mom. "I need to talk to Michael alone."

"But I need to talk to you as well," Josie tutted. She stamped her foot. "It's really important."

"Later," said Mom, trying not to sound harsh.

But that was how Josie took it, harshly. "Oh!" she huffed. "It's always Michael! Michael. Michael. Michael. Michael!" She tossed back her hair and headed for the stairs.

"Well?" Mom said as calmer air settled. The room seemed to shrink beneath her wounded gaze.

"Mom, I swear, I didn't do it."

"They've suspended you. Again."

"It's not fair. I didn't *do* it."

She raised the letter as if to form a cup for any tears she might shed. "Then why am I holding this? It says you were one of a group of boys who were known to be at the library last night. What's going on, Michael? What's happened to my beautiful, good-natured son?"

I could have gone either way at that point. I could have thrown a tantrum and stormed upstairs. Instead, I shuffled my feet and said, "I'm here. Honest."

She stood up slowly and held me by the shoulders. "Look up. Let me see your eyes."

They were filming with tears. And she knew, because of that, she didn't need to quiz me anymore. "This is an outrage," she whispered. "They can't suspend you without proof of involvement. Besides, you love your books. You're one of Mrs. Rowley's favorites. Why would you ever do a thing like that? Right, I'm taking you to school a bit earlier tomorrow and we'll have this out in Mr. Solomon's office."

"No, Mom."

She flapped the letter. "We have to stand up for what's right, Michael."

"I can't . . . Please. I just . . . Please, Mom, I can't."

"Shush," she said soothingly, stroking my face. "All right, we'll leave it be for now. But I shall write to Mr. Solomon. I'd only end up shoving *him* through a window if I lost my temper in his office. Then where would we be?"

On the front page of the *Holton Post*. Pity. I'd have given my yearly allowance to see Mom lay a punch on Solomon's chin. I picked up my schoolbag. "Gonna get changed."

"Just a minute. What's this?" She pulled down my collar.

Freya's scratch. It was the first time Mom had seen it. I'd forgotten I was supposed to be hiding it. I felt for the bandage; it was still in place. "It's nothing . . ."

"Mich-ael?" She was on her guard again. "Have you been fighting?"

"Only with . . . a tree." I made a cutting movement with my finger. "Branch."

"At school?"

Oops. There were trees at school, but climbing them was strictly forbidden. I could be digging myself into a hole, here. "Erm . . ."

"Only . . . this bandage. It's not the type I normally buy."

I shrugged. And, thankfully, she let it drop. Phew. She headed for the kitchen, saying, "You will work over these two days, won't you?"

"Course," I said. I had plenty of "homework" in the envelope the Bulldog had given me.

"By the way, what did Josie want, do you know?"

On cue, Josie came into the living room. "Huh, you're still here, then?"

I flicked her arm.

"Ow! Bully."

She came at me with punches I easily deflected. "Mom wants to know what you wanted her for."

"Oh, yeah." End of fight. She turned on her heels and swept into the kitchen.

I heard only parts of their conversation, which mostly consisted of Josie saying *Pleeze* and Mom replying *Devon?*

When it was over, Josie skipped back into the living room, beating her fists and whooping, "*Yes!*"

Well done, Agent Chantelle. One sister, perfectly glamoured.

I read the pages on Devon Winters. Just three, laid out in detailed sections. Devon was my sister's newest best friend. Not long in school. Clever. Musical. Everything Josie loved on TV or liked about bands or styles of clothing, Devon liked, too. *Separated at birth*, Chantelle had written, which was a good way to remember it. As far as Josie was concerned, Devon had no connection with me, and we were not to discuss the writing competition in front of her (or Mom). But for the purposes of our mission, Devon had seen me reading comics at school and asked what I was drawing. This had led to our collaboration on *Crow Girl*.

I read the whole thing five times, memorized it, and shredded it.

I was in my room when they came in from school. *Keep a low profile* was also in the notes. It wasn't long before Josie came thumping up the stairs, saying, "I've got this really great top you can try. It'll totally go with your eyes."

I took a breath and stepped out of my room, deliberately turning away from them, toward the bathroom.

"Oh, that's Michael," Josie said. "He's suspended for wrecking the school fountain."

"Really?" I heard Devon say. Her voice. Freya's voice. It lanced my heart.

I turned around and gave them the big-brother glare.

"Don't be fooled," Josie said. "He's a total wimp." She took Devon's hand and pulled her away.

We managed one quick glance. *Hi*, I mouthed.

Hi, she mouthed back.

The change was uncanny. Makeover hardly began to describe it. Her face was still pale, but then so was Josie's. There was only one thing Chantelle couldn't hide and that was the power of Freya's stare. It was there, just behind the pale blue lenses. The glower of the crow. The undead girl.

For the first time in days, I felt an itch on one side of my neck.

Freya played it to perfection. Slightly silly, slightly loud, and never pausing for more than ten seconds before saying something slightly inane. Josie was enraptured. It was a good thing I knew it was all an act or "Devon" would have been at the top of my list of irritating little girls to avoid.

Mom, like me, was faintly overwhelmed. I carried some dishes into the kitchen after dinner and she whispered, "Goodness, that pair can yap. How do they keep it up? I'm sure I wasn't like that at their age. Devon is a sweet girl, though. Older than her years. Quite savvy, really. In a funny way, she —"

"She what?" I asked. It wasn't like Mom to break off her sentences.

"Oh, nothing. Here, dry for me, will you?" She offered me a dish towel.

Which I gladly took. Any excuse to stay clear of the ten-best-boy-bands-*ever* discussion going on in the living room. I picked up a cup. "What were you going to say?"

"Nothing. Forget it. Just a silly thought." She looked out into the garden, lit gold by a low sun filtered through clouds. "How did you do today?"

"Mo-om?" I gave her my best hard stare.

She pulled on a pair of yellow gloves and paddled the dishwater into suds. "All right, but promise me you won't be upset?"

"I promise."

She held her breath for a second. "Devon reminds me a little bit of Freya."

My tongue could not have turned drier if I'd stuffed the whole dish towel into my mouth.

Mom saw my shock and immediately went into flappy-hand mode, spraying the plants on the windowsill with suds. "Ohhh, I knew I shouldn't have said that. Let's change the subject to something more cheerful. Let's talk about . . . soccer, eh?"

"Mom, you hate soccer. Why do you think she's like Freya?" Mom's logic would never let her mind accept that it really was Freya beneath the disguise; all the same it was worrying that she'd made the connection. I glanced nervously into the living room. The girls had reached the top three of their boy band list.

"I'm not sure," Mom said. "Her voice, a little. But more her wit. I know they're basically talking nonsense, but if you separate them out, Devon is a bit ahead of Josie — just like Freya was that time she came for tea. I liked that about her. She was a very smart girl."

Yes, she was. I put the cup down.

"Oh, this is getting worse," Mom tutted. For once, because her gloves were wet, she couldn't hug me as she liked. But it didn't stop her planting her wrists on my shoulders and unloading the big-eyed sympathy gaze. "Sorry, Michael."

"I'm fine, Mom. Really." I gently shrugged her off.

At that moment, Josie popped her head around the door. "Me and Devon are going upstairs to make her bed."

"All right," Mom said, quickly calling after her, "Josie, if Devon needs more pillows, there are some in the linen closet."

"Where?" came a distant voice from the stairs.

"The LINEN closet! Do you know how to use the pump for the airbed?"

"The what?"

"The — Oh, never mind. I'll come." Mom peeled off her gloves. She was almost out of the kitchen when she checked back and took something off the fridge door, an envelope clamped by a magnetic penguin. "What's the rule about pockets?"

"Pockets?"

"If you drop a jacket on your bedroom floor, you want it washed, right?"

"Um . . . yeah."

"So what's the rule about pockets?"

I rolled out the line. "Empty them first."

She pressed the envelope to my chest and put the magnet back. "In my experience, letters read better if they haven't been through a spin cycle of twelve hundred revolutions a minute."

She hurried out.

Tutting, I tore open the envelope. Inside was a single sheet of paper. On the paper was some printed text. All around the text were drawings of soldiers. Faceless soldiers, like on the Tommy cards. I fell back against the fridge when I saw the first line.

Alexander liked to draw.

So it was *Alexander* who'd put the envelope through my door. He had sent me a story. Or what looked like a story. I felt weak and sank down on a stool to read it.

Alexander liked to draw. It was something he had always done from the moment he could remember picking up a pencil. He began with Mommy and Daddy, in a funny house with wobbly windows and a pigtail of smoke curling out of the chimney. There were flowers in the garden, and a spiky yellow sun in the sky. And there was Dexy, the big black Labrador, chasing a ball up the street. Sometimes, Alexander drew good things, like the time when Dexy delivered five puppies into a basket in the corner of the kitchen. And sometimes he drew bad things, like the time when Mommy and Daddy argued. Then his pictures were of dinner plates smashing against walls. Daddy with his mouth wide open, shouting. Dexy hiding underneath a chair. But then Daddy went away to join an army, to fight in a foreign war. There was quiet then. A fragile peace. Mother — she didn't like to be "Mommy" — cooked for Alexander, tidied up for him, and talked to herself all day. Dexy regrew her missing fur, which was caused by stress, said Dr. Sammons, the vet. And Alexander continued to draw. He sketched and he sketched. On anything he could find. But now his pictures were not of funny houses. He drew what was not there. What lay behind his eyes. He drew what could not be seen. He drew his father.

I shuddered and folded the story away. Then I leaned into the sink and heaved. I slid down onto the floor with the acid taste of vomit in my mouth. I couldn't decide what had scared me most: the weirdness of the story or the fact that Alexander wanted me to read it or that he somehow knew my name. But

I quickly realized it was none of these things. What really clawed at my nerves was that me and this madman had something in common.

We had both gone through a family trauma.

A trauma that had left us with an absent father.

I didn't have a chance to show the piece to Freya. I saw her only once more before she and Josie went to bed. She was wearing Josie's spare bathrobe and had a hot water bottle under one arm, a teddy bear under the other. They'd braided each other's hair. Weird. "Night," I said. "Sleep well . . . Devon."

No discussion about what we would do if "the Boffin" turned up in the middle of the night. No mention of the comic she was supposed to have written. And despite the fact I'd checked my phone a dozen times, no instructions from Klimt, either. Too bad. I was tired. I let it go. Within an hour, I was in bed myself.

But I couldn't sleep.

The night was still. No rain. A faint breeze.

The usual shadows.

I just couldn't sleep.

At 2:39 a.m., I threw back the sheets and sat for a minute on the side of my bed. The house was silent. All I could hear was the tick of my clock.

I went to the window and peered out carefully. No crows. No one under the streetlamp. No flying pencils.

No Alexander.

But there was still Freya.

I crept along the landing to Josie's room, my heartbeats louder than my barefoot steps.

The door was slightly open.

Gently, I opened it a little wider.

Josie was in bed, her cute little face to the wall, asleep. But the bed on the floor, Freya's airbed, was empty.

In the silence of the night, I heard my heart thump.

I moved along the landing with a growing sense of urgency. The bathroom door was also ajar. I listened, but Freya wasn't there.

Maybe, I told myself, she'd gone downstairs for a glass of water.

Maybe she sleepwalked.

Or maybe she'd *flown*.

I slipped by Mom's room and took the stairs on tiptoe, checking the front door as I passed.

Locked.

She wasn't in the living room. She wasn't in the kitchen. The back door was chained and bolted. That left one more room to check.

Dad's old study.

I turned the handle as if I were defusing a bomb, so silent a cat would not have stirred. Dad's room, like mine, often filled with moonlight. His green leather chair was the first thing I saw, high-backed, turned toward the alcove desk. This, I was sure, would be where I'd find Freya, curled up in a ball or nesting like a crow.

I put my hand on the chair and turned it.

Empty.

"Looking for me?"

"Jeez!" I nearly broke the high-jump record.

She was behind me in the shadows at ground level, a glint of silver along one shin. As my eyes adjusted to the light, I saw she was sitting cross-legged on the floor, wearing a simple nightgown.

"What are you doing?" I hissed.

"What are you?" she replied.

"If Mom wakes up, she'll —"

"Your mom's not gonna wake up," she cut in.

Another missed beat. "If you've done anything —"

"Like what, Michael?"

The lack of trust hovered like dust motes in the moonlight.

"Sit down," she said.

"No. It's too risky. Go back to bed."

"What for? I don't sleep now. I never sleep. I have you to thank for that."

I slapped my hands to my head. This was *so* not a good idea. Why had Klimt ever sanctioned this?

She took hold of her ankle and pulled one foot in tighter to her body. "Why don't you stop being a drama queen and sit down and talk to me?"

"This was my dad's old room," I snapped, making it sound like she'd broken a rule by even daring to ruffle the carpet.

"I know," she said plainly.

"Josie told you?"

"She didn't need to. I can feel your dad's auma."

"His what?"

"Auma. It's an Inuit word for fire, but in my world, we use it to describe someone's life force. It's all over the house, but it's strongest in here." Her gaze panned the ceiling.

Okay. Now she had my attention. I dropped to her level and knelt on the floor. "Seriously? You think Dad *haunts* this place?"

"No. That's way too simple. It's more like I hear his consciousness knocking, as if he's tapping on the wrong side of frosted glass." She swiveled her eyes to focus on a single point behind me.

I looked over my shoulder. Her gaze had come to rest on the alcove wall. "The print? What about it?"

"Something's drawing me to it."

"Like what?"

She frowned. "I don't know. Go and look."

Sighing, I stood up and switched on the desk light. It burned with a smell of ancient dust. I looked over *The Tree of Life*, remembering how Klimt had been moved when he saw it. It was such a peculiar, dreamlike picture. So many whirling, twisting branches. That single black bird, so prominent among them.

"Take it off the wall," Freya said darkly.

"What for?"

"Just do it, Michael."

She sounded croaky. Crowlike. Scary. So much for Preeve and his wonder gas. Fearful of what might happen if I didn't, I put my hands around the frame and lifted the picture clear of its hook. For one moment, I thought it might be hiding a safe. But all it revealed was a brighter rectangle of the wallpaper pattern.

"Bring it closer," said Freya.

"Why? There's nothing here. It's just a stupid picture."

But I was wrong. Spectacularly wrong. As I thrust it toward her, an envelope dropped off the back of the frame and landed on the seat of the green leather chair.

I stared at it for two or three seconds before resting the print against the alcove wall. I opened the envelope. It wasn't sealed. Inside was a square of folded paper. On it was a handwritten message:

In New Mexico: Dragons abound

I almost gagged as I read it. And yet a more startling discovery awaited me. For the envelope, and therefore the message it contained, was not addressed to me or anyone in my family. Indented on the front, in fading pencil, were two letters, *L* and *N*. I knew only one person with those initials.

Liam Nolan.

Rafferty's father.

The man who helped UNICORNE with medical issues.

Dad's doctor.

My knees gave way and I sank into the chair. In the space of just a few hours, I'd had a message from a lunatic and now one from Dad.

I couldn't stop shaking as I read it aloud.

Freya didn't respond.

I gave it half a second and looked over my shoulder. She was no longer in the room. But on the floor where she'd been sitting was what looked like a comic.

Our comic.

I told myself I should probably go after her. But I couldn't find the will to get out of the chair. I read the message three times over, just to be sure I wasn't dreaming. Dragons. New Mexico. Liam Nolan. Then I picked up the comic and took it to the desk. And I sat in my father's green office chair, trying to make sense of all that was happening, and read the story of the Amazing Crow Girl and the Unicorn Boy.

It was short, just two pages long, mapped out in squares of varying sizes. Scratchy drawings. Tortured. Stark. In pencil, mostly, with the odd dash of color.

It told the story of how Unicorn Boy, eager to possess the power of flight, had lured a hostile crow to his cave by crying in the voice of a dying dragon. Trapping the bird in a *nest of promises*, he cut off its wings with the horn he had stolen from an evil unicorn. Only then did he see that the crow, now slain, had changed into a beautiful dark-haired girl. She lay dead in his arms, her *mauve* heart glowing through the skin of her breast. *What have I done?* the boy asked himself. And laying the girl on a grave marked only by a wooden cross, he kissed her forehead and turned the wicked horn on himself, pressing the point against his own dark heart, unaware that the girl's heart was beating again. . . .

It ended with the line: *To be continued . . . ?*

A question I had no answer to.

Upstairs, I found her in Josie's room, lying on the airbed, arms outstretched. On the palm of each hand lay a single black feather. And though her eyes were wide open and staring at the ceiling, I guessed she was trying to sleep.

"I'll never hurt you," I whispered.

"You will," she said. "You already have."

I looked at Josie, sleeping soundly.

Freya shut her eyes and closed her hands around the feathers.

And I shut the door softly and went back to bed, the comic in one hand, my father's cryptic message in the other.

The next morning, during a lull at breakfast, while Mom was in the kitchen and Josie had excused herself and gone to the bathroom, I showed Dad's note to Freya.

"Liam's involved," I whispered.

She nodded, not really showing much interest.

"Liam," I repeated. "Don't you think that's weird?"

She shrugged. "He was your dad's doctor. People tell doctors all sorts of stuff; they're not supposed to spill your secrets. Maybe your dad needed an outlet, is all."

"But Liam works for UNICORNE."

"So?"

"So why would Dad write a message like this? And hide it behind a picture in our house? How was Liam ever going to find it? And what does it mean? Surely, Liam knew that Dad was going on a mission to New Mexico?"

"So ask him," she said.

I intended to. I'd already tracked down the telephone number of Liam's practice and put it in my phone. Freya took a drink of orange juice and grimaced. "Yuck. Keep forgetting the undead don't like the taste of citrus."

"And there's this as well." I showed her Alexander's story and quickly explained how I'd come to find it.

"Spooky," she said. "Especially the missing father bit."

"Careful." I jerked a thumb toward the kitchen. Fortunately,

Mom had the radio on. I leaned forward and looked into Freya's blue eyes. Though I wasn't trying with any intent, I could see no telltale flecks. Maybe the undead didn't have flecks, or they couldn't be seen through colored contacts. That suddenly made me think about the different colors of the Bulldog's eyes. What if he'd been wearing contact lenses in his office? *You're skilled in the art of flecking*, he'd said, one eye continually watering. What if he'd been wearing special lenses to make me believe he was answering my questions truthfully . . . ?

"Hello, Devon calling Planet Malone."

"Uh? Sorry?"

Freya tapped her head. "You zoned out. What's up?"

"Oh, nothing." The Bulldog theory could wait for now. "Why did you leave Dad's room last night?"

She tilted her head, stringing her now-unbraided hair through her fingers. "I was tired. I'd done what I had to do. It moved you nearer to your father, didn't it?"

Or deepened the mystery further. "I don't want Klimt to know about the note. Or Alexander's story. Will you promise not to say?"

She closed her mouth and nodded. "What did you think of the comic?"

I'd been waiting for that. "The drawings were ace."

"And the story?"

"Neat, but kind of sad."

She pulled her lips in tight and looked out the window at the cloudless sky. "Like I said, no happily-ever-afters. There's not gonna be a good ending for me."

"Why did you give yourself a mauve-colored heart?"

She put a finger on a grain of toast and crushed it. "It was s'posed to be ironic. It's how they classify people with extra-sensory gifts."

I nodded, thinking back to my hourglass chat with the Bulldog. Hadn't he stamped the word *mauve* on her file? "Did Klimt tell you that?"

"Sort of."

"Meaning?"

She looked toward the kitchen. Mom was singing along to the radio. "I hear them talking when they don't think I can. Preeve, Klimt — the Bulldog when he's near. A bird's sensory powers are highly developed — especially the undead variety. MAUVE stands for Mleptran AUma VEssel. Me, you, Mulrooney, Chantelle, we all qualify. Right now, you're their number one bunny, the star at the top of their pointy tree. Your dad was probably the same when they had him."

"Vessel?"

"Human body, I guess. I don't know any more. I only hear snatches. And Preeve talks science guff most of the time. They mention the 'artifact' a lot. Don't know what that means, either. But I've heard them mention New Mexico as well. So maybe it's connected with your dad's message?"

I pulled my face into a grimace. "They sent Dad looking for dragons — apparently."

Freya lifted her shoulders. "Well, maybe he found one?"

Annoyingly, Josie burst in then. "Sorry, I was ages. Did I hear you say dragons? Is he boring you?"

Freya slipped straight into Devon mode again. "No way, José. He's been telling me about a paper chain you asked him to make for some girl who died. That's *so* sweet." She reached out and touched my hand. Hers was cold.

Josie wrinkled her nose at this show of affection. "Come upstairs. I found that clip for your hair."

"Cool!" And away they went.

I was finishing Freya's orange juice for her when Mom came in, pulling on her coat. "All done?"

"Um."

"You okay? You sound sad."

Not sad. Confused. Truth and lies. Lies and truth. Artifacts. Mauve. Dragons. New Mexico. And somewhere in the middle of it all was Dad. "I just wish I was going to school."

She found a hairbrush and tugged it through her hair. "Where are the chatty twins?"

"Upstairs."

She stepped to the door. "Josie! Devon! Two minutes! Or you're walking!"

"Coming!" they shouted.

"So is Christmas," Mom muttered. She put the brush away and strapped on her watch. "I still don't like this, Michael, you being at home alone. It's not too late for me to take the day off. I could stay here and help you study."

"I'll be all right," I said. I tilted Freya's glass between my thumb and fingers. "I might work in Dad's room if that's okay?" Maybe there were more clues waiting to be found.

She picked up her keys from a dish. "Of course it is. I'd like that. So would he."

Out of nowhere, I stood up and gave her a hug.

"Oh, Michael, I love you so much," she whispered. "We'll sort out this nonsense with the school, I promise."

Then she was yelling to the girls again.

And the sleepover was done with, and the house was at peace.

At twenty-eight minutes past nine, when I'd finally found the nerve, I called the number for Liam Nolan's office.

"Poolhaven House," a woman's voice said.

I ran my fingers over the note in my lap. "Can I speak to Dr. Nolan, please?"

"You want to make an appointment?"

"No. I just want to talk to him."

"I'm afraid that's not possible without an appointment. Are you unwell?"

"No. It won't take long. I need to speak to him about my father."

"Is your father unwell?"

"No. He's . . ."

"Are you okay?" she said kindly, filling my pause. "Only, you sound very young and really quite anxious. Is everything all right . . . between you and your father?"

"Yes. Look, I've got to go." The UNICORNE car had pulled into our drive. "Please, will you tell Liam — I mean Dr. Nolan — I called."

"Do you know Dr. Nolan personally?"

Headlights flashed at the window.

"Yes. Tell him Mi — Tell him Thomas Malone has sent him a message."

"Thomas Malone," she repeated in the way people do when they're writing something down. "Well, Dr. Nolan's not in the office until this afternoon. I can't promise anything. Can he call you on this number?"

But by then the phone was halfway to my pocket.

And I was on my way to meet Alexander's Army.

"Here are your orders," Klimt said as Mulrooney drove me and Freya, whom we'd picked up on the way, into town. "You will go into the comic store and hand in your competition entry. You will not attempt to provoke a situation. You may converse if you wish, but if AJ or Alexander tries to detain you, be polite and say that Devon's father is waiting in the parking lot. Then leave."

"That's it?" I said. "That's all we do?"

"That is all you do," Klimt replied. "I do not want to incite them to violence. It is enough to make them aware that they still have a thread of contact with you. Note how they react to Freya — assuming, of course, they recognize her. Remember, she is Devon Winters now."

"Do I really have to face them in this?" she said, plucking at the neck of a Holton school sweater.

"You're not Lara Croft," Mulrooney said. "You heard Mr. Klimt; this is strictly low-key."

"Freya, do you have your medication?" asked Klimt.

"Yuck, it makes me heave," she complained. She broke the top off a vial of liquid and downed it in one swig. "Tell Preeve it tastes like rotten apples — not that he'd care."

"But it's working?" I asked, trying not to sound anxious. Last night in Dad's room, she'd seemed close to flipping.

She flicked her blond hair. "Devon through and through. Don't worry, I plucked my leg feathers before I came out."

"Really?"

"Mich-ael?" She made a dumb face. Okay, one point to her: Being undead hadn't "killed" her warped sense of humor.

"You have your phones?" Klimt asked.

I tapped my jeans pocket.

Freya showed him the cell phone Preeve had given her. A flashy state-of-the-art thing that would have made Josie thoroughly jealous.

"And most important, the story?"

"My story," Freya said. She snatched it off my lap. "I want to be the one who puts it in his hand."

"We're here," said Mulrooney, bringing the car to a halt.

Klimt looked at us both. "Anything else before we send you in?"

"Bottle of soda and a hand grenade?" said Freya.

Klimt graced her with a rare smile. "Michael, are you nervous? You seem withdrawn."

Hardly surprising. So much had happened in the last two days. So much I wanted to challenge him with. But this wasn't the time or place. "Let's just get it done," I said.

He nodded and the doors clicked open.

Freya jumped straight out.

Klimt put a hand on my arm. "Be careful. She is very impulsive."

Oh, like he really needed to tell me. I shook him off and stepped into the parking lot.

As we entered the mall, I looked behind me and watched the car back up and pull away. It made me wonder what Klimt did at times like this. As far as I knew, he didn't get involved in field operations. But assuming Mulrooney was part of our backup, we were too far away from the UNICORNE facility for him to drop Klimt and return to the store. So —?

"Niiiice boots," I heard Freya say.

She was looking in the window of the Comfi-Foot Shoe Store at a pair of cherry-red army-style boots. Huge laces. Heavy on leather. The sort of thing she would have worn in her goth existence. The sort of thing the Boffin wore now. I shuddered and hauled her away. "Come on. I don't think shopping was on Klimt's agenda."

"You know nothing about Klimt," she said, hooking her arm slightly venomously through mine. "Or his agenda."

"Oh? What else have you heard them saying?"

She walked on a little way, looking around at the shoppers, perhaps wondering, as I was, if there were UNICORNE agents watching us. "Nothing you couldn't have worked out for yourself."

I unhooked her arm and yanked her to a stop. "I'm tired of playing guessing games, Freya. Just tell me."

She chewed her lip, taking off a little of the light pink makeup that hid the telltale blue underneath. "All right. Pretend I've got something in my eye."

I nodded and gently pulled down on her cheek.

"Not too hard. I'm in contacts, remember?"

"Sorry. Go on." I bent my head.

"I haven't heard anything new, but I'm pretty sure I've figured out what's going on. Klimt could collar these guys any time he likes, and yet he's sending us in. I think he just wants to rate Alexander to decide how useful he might be to UNICORNE. So he's pitting him against his best Talen. The Boffin versus Unicorn Boy, aka the Reality Kid. As for Crow Girl, she's the expendable bait, thrown in to stir things up a bit. Entering the competition is just an excuse to get us in the ring."

I released her eye. "That doesn't make sense. If that was true, why would he have told us to keep this low-key?"

She waited for a mother to go past with a stroller, then set off walking again, veering away down the shopping lane that led to the far side of the mall. For a girl so slight, she covered the ground like an athlete. "If Klimt put a lightsaber in your hand and told you to challenge AJ to a fight, would you do it?"

"Um, no."

"Exactly. This is not a mission; it's an experiment, Michael. Something's going to happen in that store. Klimt is just —"

Suddenly, she stopped walking and pulled me to one side. I'd hardly noticed that we'd passed through the mall and were now on the service road, only yards from the bookstore. A colorful figure had just stepped out of The Fourth Enchantment.

AJ.

Luckily, he was walking away from us. He turned the next corner and went out of sight.

"Now what?" I whispered.

Her eyes narrowed. "If AJ's not there, Alexander must be holding down the store. I guess we're gonna meet him sooner than we thought. Let's take a look."

But when we got there, stuck on the door was a sign.

BACK IN 30 MINS

For some reason, that made me more anxious, not less.

Freya cupped her face with her hands and peered through the door. "Can't see a light."

Good. So we could leave. With one eye on the alleyway, I took out my phone. "I'm calling Mulrooney."

"Wait, I've got a better idea," she said. A grin as wide as the street lit her face. "Why don't we go in and take a look around?"

She put her shoulder to the door and it opened a crack.

"Freya, what are you *doing*? That's against the law."

"*Pff!* Some agent you are," she taunted. "It's on a catch, unlocked. I didn't *do* anything. It just . . . moved when I leaned on it. Anyway, it's no big deal. If anyone comes, we're delivering our comic. It's not as though we're going to steal anything."

"But Alexander might be upstairs."

She spread her hands. "Isn't that why we're here?"

"No. I don't like this. I'm calling — Oh, heck, shut the door. Quickly!" I'd been looking up and down the road for dangers, and one had suddenly appeared. A post office van had come out of the road AJ had turned down. It pulled up with a ratcheted brake. A post office worker jumped out, carrying a thick white envelope. "Morning," he said.

"Morning," I muttered, and stepped aside.

"Closed?" he tutted, seeing the sign. He beat the package against his palm. "That's annoying. Won't get this through his puny mail slot. I'll leave it next door."

"Actually, it's open," Freya said, pushing the door with her finger. "We're kind of keeping guard while we wait for the guy to come back."

"Well. Well done, you," the postman said. "It's nice to see some honesty in our youth. Pop this inside for me, then, will you?"

He handed the package to Freya. She glanced at it and dropped it just inside the door.

"Have a nice day," the postman said, and he got back into his van and drove away.

The moment he was out of sight, I went for my phone again. But before I could put a finger to the screen, Freya said, "Michael, there's something you need to know."

"I told you, we're leaving. I'm not taking chances."

"We don't need to. The store is empty."

I threw her a puzzled look. "How do you know?"

She opened the door again and picked up the package. "Check out who it's addressed to."

I cast my eye over the name.

"Alexander Jonathan," she said.

"AJ," I whispered.

She nodded slowly. "There's no one upstairs. AJ was fooling you; he *is* Alexander. He's the Boffin."

Scared hardly began to describe it. Sick. Weak. Slightly light-headed. That was how I felt as I began to put the pieces together. The noises I'd heard from upstairs last time I'd been in the store must have been AJ flexing his mind, picturing his army standing at attention or turning on the radio. He wasn't just duping me, he was chalking up a kind of smug victory, telling me the truth in a weird sort of way. Alexander Jonathan *was* upstairs — or at least that projection of his mind was. On top of all this, there was also the Boffin, the spooky, comic book villain Alexander became when he ran the big opera-tions, like moving the library cart or blowing the streetlamp outside my window. I looked at the address again and wanted to run, but Freya was psyched up and ready to roll; she had already melted into the store.

"Freya!" Even if AJ wasn't here, to be caught inside would be a big mistake. I double-checked the street. An ash-red pigeon was strutting about, pecking at a patch of crushed potato chips. Where, I wondered, could UNICORNE be? I could see no obvious hiding places, and the windows opposite were boarded up. It felt very much like we were on our own here.

"This is so cool," I heard Freya say.

With one last look outside, I stepped into the store and pulled the door shut. A ray of sunlight through the postered window had carved the room into splintered shadows, giving us some weird silhouettes for company, but also some low-level light. Freya was walking around the boxes, dragging her fingers over the comics. "Look at all these. I'd like this place if it wasn't run by a wacko."

"Freya —?"

"Okay, let's get busy." She pirouetted and moved to the back of the store, then slipped behind the counter and dropped out of sight, rustling around like a mouse in a wastepaper basket. I checked the time. Five minutes since we'd seen AJ leave. For now, at least, we were safe.

"Nothing much here," Freya reported. "Just paperwork and an old banana skin. Ow!" As she stood up, she bumped her head on the counter. It was then I saw the Tommy doll. It was sitting against the cash register, lit by a spot from the rear window, its cone-shaped head lolling off to one side. Suddenly, an arm sprang sideways.

I gasped so loudly, even Freya squealed a little. "What?"

"The doll. It moved."

She picked it up and played with the limbs. "Don't be dumb. It was me, banging the counter. AJ's not here, remember?" She tapped the doll's head and put it back.

I still shuddered. "It gives me the creeps, that thing. Look, leave our comic on the counter and let's just —" My words dried up and the sentence fell away. I tried to swallow, but it seemed as if my tongue had grown to the size of a small pillow.

In the stairwell, a light had clicked on.

"He's here," I whispered.

"How?" said Freya.

"A back entrance. I don't know. Let's go."

"Chill out," she shushed, stepping away from the counter. "I'd sense him if he was here. It's probably one of those movement detector things." And before I could stop her, she'd gone to the bottom of the stairs and shouted, "HELLO?!"

No response.

As she turned back to me, the light clicked off. "See?"

I wasn't convinced. I looked at the Tommy doll. It had slipped into a floppy heap of limbs. "This is too weird," I said.

"Well, man up, 'cause it's gonna get worse." She took a coin from her pocket. "Heads or tails?"

"What are we flipping for?"

"Who stands guard and who goes upstairs."

"No, Freya! We've done what we needed to do. Let's just go."

"And tell Klimt what? That you had the chance to go up a floor but didn't?"

She flipped the coin and trapped it on the counter.

"Heads," I said reluctantly.

She lifted her hand. "Typical. Heads. Your choice."

I picked the upstairs, mainly because I didn't trust her not to disturb stuff. The basic agreement was this: She would stand outside the store and keep watch, with my number cued up on her phone. If AJ appeared, all she had to do was set my phone ringing and I would have time to hurry downstairs. Then one of us would tell him we'd found the door open and we hoped he didn't mind but we'd put our competition entry on the counter.

Then we'd leave.

Simple.

The light clicked on as I took the first step. The stairs were wide and bowing with age. Both sides were lined with stacks of old comics, the layers slipping against each other like a glacier making its way to the sea. Halfway up was a small square landing where the stairs doglegged away to the right. At the top of the steps was a poky bathroom with an old-fashioned toilet with a tank high up on the wall, painted green. It didn't smell good. Water was dripping onto the floor, eating a sagging hole in the boards. Even here, there were posters of comic book heroes. I turned away, pinching my nose. It would have taken something heroic to cure that smell.

Opposite the bathroom was a single-bed room, messy with clothes and unwashed dishes. Yet more comics were spilled around the floor. A wardrobe with a broken hinge stood next to a door that seemed to lead out to a fire escape. AJ's trademark bow ties were arranged around an arched mirror propped against the wall, clipped to its edges like sleeping butterflies. I passed by that room as well and crept along a landing, into the room that would be over the shop. Like the bedroom, it was small and untidy, bursting with dusty storage boxes and comics piled up in ceiling-high columns. There were makeshift shelves full of figurines, too, and an old kitchen cabinet stuffed with rolled-up posters. I was about to turn away and go back to Freya, when I caught a glint of a metal stair between the boxes. It led to an open hatch in the ceiling. Another room. An attic.

By now, I was thinking I had done enough. How much farther did I want to go? The answer, of course, just knocked and knocked. Up, Michael. If there's anything to find, it will be in the attic.

But I couldn't stop thinking of scary movies I'd watched with Dad. How we'd loved to shout at the screen together.

"Don't go out into the garden!" "Don't turn that handle!" "Don't push that button!"

Don't go up those stairs.

But I did.

Using the light from my phone to guide me, I climbed the ladder and eased through the hatch. The roof space was high enough to comfortably stand up in. It could not have been more different from the rooms below. No clutter. No damp. No nasty smells. Although the rafters were visible, the joists were boarded. They led, like a catwalk, to a table against the gable wall. An office chair stood in front of it, an aluminum wastebasket just to one side, half-full of scrunched-up paper. On the table was a sloping board, the kind of thing an artist or designer might use. It was lit by a bent-over halogen light. On it was a drawing of a faceless soldier. He was holding a flamethrower.

On the wall behind the table was a huge bulletin board covered with spreads from a comic book in development. Each spread was labeled with a page number and the title *Alexander's Army.* It told, in graphic form, the story AJ had left under my door. There was his father, throwing plates at walls, beating the dog, shouting at his cowering son to stand up straight and act like a man, the face drawn so grotesquely close that it was possible to count the drops of spit flying off the man's tongue.

There was more. The story continued, beyond the part AJ had sent me. It showed how his teacher, Mrs. Roop, had found Alexander in a corner of the classroom with his head hunched over a notebook, drawing.

Is that a soldier? she asked. It was one of the faceless Tommies, its trousers cut off at the midpoint of the shin, held up by a pair of suspenders. A coil of rope was slung around one of its shoulders, its booted feet splayed wide apart.

Why does it have no features? she asked. She looked concerned. Her hand was partly covering her mouth.

Alexander kept on drawing.

In the next frame, Mrs. Roop asked another worried question: *Is everything all right at home, dear?*

And Alexander replied, *Dog's got fleas.* The next frame showed him pulling up his trouser leg to reveal a bite mark, red and blotchy.

Are you treating him? the teacher said. *Spraying him with anything?*

There the drawings ended. But next to them was a paragraph of printed text:

Alexander shrugged. He thought about fleas and their horrible little bites. They itched. They kept him awake at night. They made him rub his shin with the heel of his shoe. Then his trousers got dirty and Mother would shout. Fleas were bad, Alexander decided. Fleas were a problem that needed to be sprayed. He looked at his drawing, at the gap between the soldier's trousers and boots. He made a mark on the bare skin with his pencil. Gave the man a flea bite. There, it was done. Now the army had the enemy, too. And the army would know what to do about it. For a second or two, the pencil twirled in Alexander's fingers. Then he bent forward and drew what he thought would be a gun in the soldier's hands, a gun with tiny bullets for shooting fleas. But when he sat back and looked at the razzle-dazzle lines jumping out of the barrel, he knew it was something better than bullets. It was FIRE. He closed his book and put away his pencils. No more fleas in the house tonight.

I stood away, panting in fright. But the story was nothing nearly as bad as what I saw next.

On the far side of the bulletin board were some newspaper clippings bunched together in a rough kind of collage. I froze as I saw a familiar headline:

BOY IN THRILLING CLIFF-TOP RESCUE

It was a clipping from the *Holton Post*, telling the story of how I'd saved Rafferty Nolan's dog from falling off the cliffs on Berry Head. I lifted it aside and there I was, pictured holding the dog in my arms. Michael Malone. Schoolboy hero. AJ had known me even before I entered the shop.

I riffled through the rest of the clippings, taking closer note of them now. There was stuff about Rafferty from a different newspaper, and a whole bunch of articles about weird goings-on with crows, including the incident at the garden center. And buried deep among them, yellowed with age, was one that chilled me rigid.

LOCAL MAN DISAPPEARS IN MYSTERIOUS CIRCUMSTANCES

Dad. There was an article on Dad. Why was AJ collecting info on my father?

I backed away again, catching the arm of the halogen lamp. As the light shuddered around the rafters, I saw a glint of something where the angle of the roof met the wall of the building. An eye. A small dark eye.

A crow.

I thought at first it was her, Freya. But Freya would have had no reason to attack. The bird flew out of the eaves, straight at me. I flapped and beat it away with my forearm. It opened its beak but didn't produce a sound as it veered off into the shadows again. That was it. I'd seen enough. Boy, I wanted to be out of that place. From now on, Klimt could deal with it.

But I only got halfway back to the hatch.

"Hello, Michael," said a voice. "I've been expecting you."

Standing there in his boots and white coat and oversize glasses, arms angled out to his sides, was the Boffin.

Before I could scream or run or attack him, a piece of wood flew across the space between us, struck me on the forehead, and dropped me to my knees. As I folded, too dizzy to resist, the wire from a TV aerial ripped away from its pins on a rafter and wrapped itself around one wrist. Something pulled my arms behind my back and tied my wrists together with the wire. All this time, the Boffin hadn't moved. But as I started to pant and my panic level rose to a point where I knew I might make a reality shift, he crouched down in front of me and said, "Don't. I know what you are. Trust me, it would be the last thing you did. The girl would die and you'd never get to hear what I know about your father."

Even then, half-dazed, I tried to play the game. "Don't know what you're talking about."

"One word: Bulldog," he whispered.

I dribbled some saliva, which instantly annoyed him. *"Company, clear that up!"* he barked, aiming his words into the space beside us. I thought I heard a patter of booted feet and what sounded like a ladder being erected. Right before my eyes, a tissue jumped out of a box on the desk and skittered across the boards. It dabbed at the spill, then scrunched itself up and flew away into the darkness. "*Litter!*" he shouted. Adding weirdly, "*It does matter, Hodges! Ten laps. The lot of you. I've told you before, discipline is everything. Dissent will not go unpunished.*"

And the whole attic drummed to the eerie sound of running.

The Boffin grabbed my chin. Behind the lenses of his glasses, his eyes swam like fish in a bowl. "You must at least be intrigued, Michael? *Grimper! Lift your feet or you'll go ten more!*"

"What do you want?" I panted.

"Revenge," he said plainly.

"Why, what have I done?"

"You, nothing. And if you do as I say, you won't be harmed. It's him I want, your boss, the top dog. I thought the girl would be my ticket. But I was wrong; *you're* the real prize, aren't you?"

"If you've hurt her, I'll . . ."

"*Company, HALT!*"

With a quick *chuk-chuk* of boots, the invisible army stopped running.

The Boffin released his grip on my chin. "*Find his phone. Quickly.*"

He blinked his eyes once. With great force, my jeans pocket was ripped from its seams. My phone tumbled out, along with some coins. He picked up the phone and started tapping the screen. "Why don't we call her? She must be getting cold outside. And look, it's beginning to rain." He snapped his fingers and a blind rattled back on a sloping skylight. Heavy spots of water were crowning the glass. "Or perhaps we'll send Charlie to keep her company?" He held out an arm and made clicking noises. The crow fluttered onto his wrist, teetering as it landed. "What do you say, Michael? Shall we invite the Amazing Crow Girl to our party?"

"You're crazy," I snapped.

He smiled again. "So would you be if you knew what they'd made me do."

"Who?"

"Michael, Michael," he tutted. He tapped the phone again and brought up an avatar of Chantelle, a pic I'd taken when she wasn't looking. "This is one of their agents. Pretty, isn't she? Wouldn't show Freya if I were you."

"Let me go. Freya will come looking for me any minute."

With a spare finger, he stroked the crow's wing. The bird tried to caw as it strutted restlessly along his arm. "Hear that, Charlie? She's going to come looking. Your beloved mistress. Your dark crow queen. The half human you've been spying on for me. What is it, eh? What's making you hop? Are you sensing her now? On the stairs, perhaps? Perhaps she's hiding in the bathroom, ready to spring."

"FREYA!" I shouted as loudly as I could. "FREYA, HE'S GOT ME! RUN!"

No response. No shout back or sound of retreat.

The Boffin smiled, but this was no friendly chewing-gum grin. There was no sign of the bow-tied AJ on this side of his split personality. "No cavalry," he said. "So what's upsetting Charlie boy, eh?"

He pushed his arm forward.

"No!" I cried, thrashing around as the bird flew at me.

"*Company, hold him,*" the Boffin growled.

Instantly, the invisible army pulled me down flat, almost trapping the crow beneath my arm.

"*BE CAREFUL!*" he thundered as Charlie spread his wings. "*That bird's worth more than twenty of you. What was that, Dobbs? You horrible little man. You break one feather off that tail and I'll put you in a hole so deep the sky will be reduced to a single dot.*"

I felt the pinch of claws on my shoulder. "Get it off me!" I yelled as the beak jabbed my neck, close to the area where Freya had scratched me. Charlie nipped twice at the bandage, then ripped it off, exposing the wound beneath. I yelped as he pecked the scar. A warm wet trail ran under my collar.

"Enough," said the Boffin, flapping Charlie away. He pressed a thumb to the skin beside the cut. "Tainted you, hasn't she? Darkened your blood. Perhaps she wants you to join her, Michael? So you can rule the crows together. Or am I being too romantic?"

"What do you *want*?" I screamed. Why couldn't I cause a shift and put *him* in a hole? But in a small and diminishing part of my mind, I already knew the answer to that. He was holding me at bay with a thread of hope, just as Klimt and the Bulldog had done. He clearly knew about UNICORNE. And that meant there was a chance he was telling the truth, that he really did know something about Dad.

He stood up and walked to the desk. "You're going to help me get to the Bulldog. In a moment, you'll call them and say you've accelerated your reality, defeated Alexander, and the army is destroyed. *Shut up, Hodges. It's a ploy, you fool.* They do know about the army, I take it? I've left enough clues by now."

"What do you mean, 'accelerated my reality'?"

He sighed deeply. "*Grimper, give him a reminder of what we can do.*"

"Agh!" I felt a sudden pain in my calf. "Grimper" was pulling the hairs from my legs. I let him take three before I cried, "Enough!"

"*Stand down,*" the Boffin muttered.

"Ow!" Another hair went.

"Grimper, STAND DOWN! Or it's solitary again!"

Fighting my wrist ties, I squirmed around and looked at the Boffin. A bead of sweat was glistening on his brow. Was it my imagination, or was the part of his mind that commanded the army becoming difficult to control? "All right. I know about the reality shifts. I've just never heard anyone say 'accelerated' before."

"Interesting. Not part of the DNA program yet but still a Talen to be reckoned with. Your father trained you, then? Chip off the old block and all that?"

"What do you *know* about my dad?!"

He moved his head to one side, cracking a bone in the back of his neck. "Quick reminder of the rules here, Michael. When I ask a question, you answer me. *Grimper . . .*"

"NO!" I pulled up my legs. "Dad didn't teach me the reality shifts. It just happens. I . . . I can't control it. Please tell me what you know. How do you even know about the Bulldog?"

Too late. A wild flapping in the darkness claimed his attention.

And then I heard what Charlie had sensed: Freya, in the rooms below, calling.

"Michael? Where are you? What are you doing? It's nearly time. And I'm sure I can sense him." She was close, somewhere near the storage room.

"FREYA, RUN!" I screamed as loudly as I could.

"*Company!*" the Boffin roared. He clenched his fists and squeezed his eyes shut.

I heard a squeal and a door slammed below, followed by thumping and Freya's muffled shouts.

The Boffin relaxed. He staggered a little as though the effort had proved too much. "Now she's where she should be — caged," he said.

From the rough direction of her calls, I guessed he'd trapped her in the stinking bathroom.

"No more talk," he said, bringing the phone to my ear. "Make the call, just as I said, or I introduce the girl to my latest recruit." He nodded at the flame-throwing soldier on the board. "Private Keeble is keen to demonstrate his loyalty — *unlike some I could mention!* In case you don't know already, Michael, there's only one thing the undead fear: fire."

"No . . ."

"Number," he growled. "Which of these bogus contacts is him?"

I shook my head. "I don't have the Bulldog's number."

"I'm not dealing with the French girl or the Marine. Three seconds, then Keeble goes down the ladder."

"All right! I can go higher than them. AK. Dial AK."

The initials didn't seem to mean anything to him, but if what I was planning was going to work, they very soon would.

He brought up Klimt's number. "No tricks. Tell them what I said if you want the girl to live." He let the phone ring. Klimt answered immediately.

"Michael?"

"Yes. Listen carefully. I'm in the attic in Alexander's store. You can probably tell from the TONE of my voice that I've been in a fight. You know that TONE, don't you, Klimt?"

Behind his glasses, the Boffin's eyes twitched. I was pretty sure he knew I was up to something, but fortunately Klimt had gotten the message.

"I know it," he said. "Do you want to hear it?"

"Yes."

Right away, a pulse of sound came from the phone. It ran down my ear and exploded like a firework deep in my brain. Klimt had tested this procedure on my previous mission, so I knew exactly what to expect. Somehow, the pulse vibrated my senses, allowing a "ghost" form of me to detach from my body and work on a separate plane of consciousness. The ghost could move at the speed of thought, which meant that time on the physical plane was effectively stopped. It had worked then and it worked again now. I peeled away from the Michael on the floor and saw the Boffin crouched beside me with the phone in his hand, absolutely still.

Perfect.

During my previous mission, I'd seen things move on the physical plane when a ghost had brushed by them. So I quickly knelt by my hands, hoping I could untie myself. Success. The rope moved. But as I worked the knot loose, I heard an echoey click, and something cold touched the side of my head. I turned with a gun pressed hard to my temple.

In front of me were ten or a dozen faceless soldiers.

"Move any furver an' you die," one of them said.

I glanced down at the name on his combat jacket.

DOBBS.

They looked exactly like they did on the Tommy cards, but now in full 3-D, like a Japanese manga comic come to life. A unit of soldiers, dressed as they might have been in World War I. When they spoke, lines appeared on their faces. Horizontal dashes for the eyes and mouth, a single vertical dash for the nose. When the words came out, the mouth line broke into a wavy pattern. In size, they were small, probably no taller than halfway up my shin. Yet due, perhaps, to the strange conditions of the plane we were on, they never seemed out of proportion to me. They were dressed identically in army boots and combat gear, including those familiar rounded helmets. The only quick way to tell them apart was by the name badges stitched on their jackets or by the things they carried. Dobbs, for instance, had a coil of rope and a grappling hook around one shoulder. Grimper had a rose tattoo on his forearm. Clegg had an old-fashioned military rifle and a double grenade pouch fixed to his belt. Hodges had a pistol, still at my head. They seemed to be the main four. There was no clear leader, but Dobbs was the one doing most of the talking.

"State yer name an' rank, soldier."

"I-I'm not a soldier," I stuttered.

"You 'eard 'im. Name an' rank," said Hodges. He pushed the gun again.

Part of me was thinking this couldn't be happening. That if I closed my eyes and concentrated hard, these strange little men would pop like bubbles or float away. The army, I kept telling myself, was a figment of Alexander's imagination. He'd created them *in his mind*. Yet they seemed capable of acting independently. It was impossible to think they could fire live bullets, but the barrel at my head felt scarily real and I wasn't going to take any chances.

"M-Malone," I said. "You know who I am."

"We know 'im," said Dobbs. He pointed at my motionless physical body. "But you're like us. 'Ow'd you get 'ere?"

"I can . . . switch," I said, making it up as I went along. "I can go back to . . . him at any moment."

Instantly, half the men leveled a rifle, as if all they had to do was think they were armed and, *bing*, it happened.

"Not if you want to keep breathin'," said Hodges.

I floated my hands in surrender. "Don't shoot. I'm not ready to go back yet. I . . . I need to get away from the Boffin."

Dobbs took a step forward. "Now, ain't that a funny thing? So do we."

So they weren't quite free of Alexander after all. "I don't understand. You're part of him. He created you. He commands you, doesn't he?"

A ripple of laughter ran around the troop.

"He's losin' it," said Dobbs. "Can't 'andle us no more." He tapped the side of his helmet. *Dink, dink, dink.* "Finks too much. We need 'im out of the picture."

"How?"

He drew a line across his neck.

Dead? His own men wanted him *dead?* "But if he dies, surely you'll die, too?"

"Not if you take us wiv yer," Dobbs said. His mouth made an O shape. "When you switch." He gestured at Hodges, who lowered his gun.

Me, take *them?*

Me, command Alexander's Army?

"That's impossible," I said. "That can't . . . happen." And even if it could, it was a chilling thought, stealing another man's imagination. What would that do to Alexander's head? What would it do to *mine?*

Dobbs sniffed, making his nose line wiggle. "Keeble!" he shouted. "Get down 'ere!"

My eyes drifted to the table. Almost magically, the drawing of the flame-throwing soldier grew out of the board. He jumped onto a chair, then shinnied down a leg to the floor and came running to join the others. Strapped to his back was a cradle carrying two tall cylinders, which were connected to a flexible hose and a gun nozzle. "Sir! Yes, sir!"

Grimper tilted his helmet back. "'Ark at the new boy, givin' it the 'sirs.' We're all one 'ere, soldier. No one gives the orders. Ain't that right, *Dobbs*?"

"Don't 'urt to 'ave a bit of direction," Dobbs argued.

"That's not what we agreed," said Grimper.

Clegg backed Dobbs up. "Wivout command, we're ragged, Grimps."

But Hodges was in the Grimper camp. "We can decide who barks and who jumps when we're free. I say we run wiv the boy."

"All agreed?" Dobbs said.

"Aye!" said the company.

All except Grimper, who stared at me doubtfully and tumbled a coin across his knuckles.

Dobbs said, "Cut us from the Boffin. Now."

I shook my head. "No. I won't kill him."

Despite his lack of facial expressions, I could tell that Dobbs was growing impatient. He said to Keeble, "I take it that thing works, soldier?"

Keeble triggered the gun. A strange orange cloud billowed out of the nozzle, making the razzle-dazzle shape Alexander had described in his story. I could feel it had heat, but in texture, it was like a foamy marzipan, as though Alexander hadn't pictured it completely or the effect was limited by the suspension of time. It left sparks that glowed on the boards all the same. Maybe fire could cross the life planes. Certainly, Dobbs seemed to think it could.

He said to Keeble, "Torch the bathroom. Place stinks, anyway."

"Stop!" I shouted. And not only did Keeble stay put, he also stood at attention. Two of the lesser men did the same. Was this the clue to them, I wondered, direct and forceful command? "All right, I'll help you — but I want him alive. He's got information I need. The girl has to go free as well."

"I told yer," Dobbs said, pointing at the Boffin, "if 'e lives, we can't move on."

"You can," I bluffed. "My . . . boffins have all the latest technology. They'll make the swap work without killing him. When it's done, I'll set you free."

"I don't trust 'im," said Grimper. "I can smell the crow on 'im. Let's finish 'im and wait for a better chance. He's just a snotty kid. What use would 'e be to us, anyway?"

But Dobbs wanted to hear the whole story. "'Ow you plannin' to take 'im prisoner?"

"Let me tie his hands. When I'm back in my body, I'll call my . . . unit. They'll storm the building and capture him."

The men looked at one another. Clegg fingered his collar. Grimper tumbled his coin the opposite way. "The Boffin don't need 'ands to command us."

"I know. But if you follow my . . . order, he'll be harmless."

"Let's 'ear it," said Dobbs. "What's yer order?"

"It's easy," I said, trying not to gulp or show any sign of weakness. "You disobey him."

"What?" said Grimper.

"When I switch back to my body and he finds out he's bound, he'll try and use you to hurt me, won't he?"

"Go on," said Dobbs.

"He's powerless if you refuse."

"Mutiny?" said Hodges.

The word dominoed around the other men.

"That's dirty," said Clegg.

"Risky," said Grimper.

But Dobbs was slowly nodding his head. His eye lines tilted and twitched, as if I'd flicked a switch and he'd somehow grown in confidence — and power. I shivered, fearful of what I'd started. As I watched Dobbs working through my plan, I realized why they hadn't mutinied already. Clegg was right. Without command, they were a mess. Dangerous, certainly, but indecisive. They couldn't stage a proper coup until the directive was actually given — a weakness Alexander must have recognized and struggled to keep out of his crazy mind. In giving them the order to disobey him, I had broken through that barrier and taught them the idea of insurrection. Dobbs was calculating new possibilities. The army had moved forward in its quest for liberation — and I had made a terrible mistake.

Trying to regain some control, I said, "Are we agreed? The Boffin is my prisoner?"

Dobbs ignored me. "Sparks!" he snapped.

One of the rear rank stepped forward. "Yeah?"

"What 'appens if we rake that light downstairs? The dodgy one on the flakin' cord?"

"The wirin' blows and it all goes up."

A new pattern appeared on Dobbs's mouth. A horrible malicious smile. "You 'ear that, lads? It all goes up."

"So *we* kill the Boffin?" Grimper said.

Dobbs nodded. He started to chew an invisible stick of gum. "Yeah. An' you know what, lads? I reckon if *we* do it, we cut *ourselves* free."

"No!" I shouted. "Abandon the mission!"

"Mission stands," said Dobbs.

Stands, the men echoed. *Stands. Stands.* Their feet began to pound in rhythm to the words.

"I'm not your enemy!" I said. "If you burn the place, I won't get out!"

And neither would Freya.

"Then we'll make it quick fer yer," said Dobbs. He turned to the riflemen. "Aim between his eyes, lads. Ready . . ."

A black unicorn. Klimt had taught me that the way to return to my body was to concentrate my mind on the UNICORNE symbol. Just before Dobbs could finalize his order, I pictured the rearing black horse with its tail looped into a letter *e*. And . . .

. . . *Wham!* I came back with a hefty jolt. The Boffin was still crouched beside me, holding the phone to my ear. But now I had the advantage of surprise and also of knowing that my hands were untied. In the confusion, I moved quicker than he did. Grabbing the wood he'd used against me, I struck him across the shoulders with my baseball swing. Bang. Home run. He went down, groaning. I hovered over him, shaking for a second, wondering if I should hit him again. But acts of violence had always sickened me; rescuing Freya was all that mattered now. So I dropped the wood and ran for the hatch, thinking I had done enough.

I was wrong.

As I reached the opening, comics began flying up through the hole. I laid my arms across my face and tried to force a way through. But they came like a swarm of angry bees, and all I could do was stagger back into the attic. And it wasn't just comics. A storm of pencils and other drawing objects rained against the back of my head and neck, stinging where they caught a point of bare skin. Even the wastebasket bounced off my shoulder and went spinning like tumbleweed into the eaves. Far from disobeying the Boffin's orders, the army was cooperating fully again, angry, no doubt, that I'd escaped. I heard a rolling noise, and the next thing I knew, the office chair had sped across the boards and smacked the soft tissue at the back of my knees. It scooped me up like the jaws of a digger and took me on a giddy ride before stopping suddenly and spilling me out. My head cracked against a beam and I almost passed out. I threw an arm sideways for something to hold and heard a rapid *Ching! Ching!* followed by dozens more. *Ching! Ching! Ching!* Before I knew it, I couldn't move. Amazingly, he'd used a staple gun to pin my jacket sleeve to a rafter.

He staggered toward me, his hair beginning to fall out of shape — lank, the way AJ wore it. His spectacles were broken, a star of cracked glass hiding one wild eye. Blood was seeping from an unseen wound, staining the arm of his lab coat a bright raspberry color.

In a voice bristling with menace, he said, "You shouldn't have done that, Michael. We were getting on so famously, you and I. You could have left unharmed. This is not your battle. And now look where we are — *You what, Dobbs?*" He stood back, swiping the air as if he'd like to dent a tin helmet with his fist. "*Stand at attention when I'm speaking to you! Straighten your back, you weedy little man! I make the decisions. And I will keep on making the decisions! See this?*" He snatched up a Tommy card from the mess on the floor. It looked like a kneeling Grimper. "*All I have to do is tear this in half and Grimper's finished.*" He made a nick in the top. "*Feel that, Grimper? Uncomfortable, isn't it? That's how close any of you are to complete obliteration. You think I couldn't draw new men if I wanted to? We have a mission and we're sticking to it. To the finish, do you hear? To the FINISH!*" I heard a thump of heels. His threats were working. For now, at least, the army was back in his grip.

"Let me go," I said, slurring the words. My head was throbbing after that bump. I pulled at the sleeve of my jacket. "That call will have warned my people I'm in trouble."

"Your people," he laughed. "I was one of 'your people' once — or did my father forget to put that in your notes? Unlike him to be careless — or do I mean devious? It all blurs into one where he's concerned. He must be old now. Sagging. Worn rough by all those years in the military."

"The Bulldog?" I gasped, catching on. The plate thrower. The dog kicker. The absent dad. The man at the head of UNICORNE. The Bulldog was Alexander's *father?*

"Father . . ." he muttered grimly. He looked down at his bloodstained hands. "I wish you could take him a message from me, but he'll understand when he rakes through the ashes that his boy is back — and gunning for him. *Company!*" He blinked his eyes shut. The table light flickered, then buzzed and went out, leaving us solely dependent on the skylight.

"What have you done?" I panted, tugging at my sleeve. Ashes. What did he mean, ashes?

"Shame to see the old place go," he said. "But it's time to redeploy the men. Pity, Michael. If you knew what a monster my father was, you'd have stayed with the plan and walked right out of here. But there's more than one way to muzzle a dog." He threw aside his lab coat and glasses and pulled on a green bow tie. "Normally, I'd lose the boots as well, but that fire escape is as slippery as sealskin in stockinged feet. And wouldn't you know, it's raining still. Can you *believe* the weather we're having? Whatever happened to the sunshine, man?"

Smoke. I smelled smoke. The store was on fire. Dobbs had gotten his wish after all. "Cut me loose!" I yelled.

He popped a stick of gum into his mouth and started chewing. From Alexander to AJ in just a few seconds. He pinged the bow tie. "Bye, Michael. They say the smoke gets you before the flames. I'll wave to the Crow Girl on my way out."

"No!" I screamed, kicking and tugging. "No! You can't leave us like this!"

"Charlie boy." He clicked his tongue.

The crow came out of the shadows, strutting in a figure eight around the boards as if it were following a trail of ants.

"Charlie!" AJ put out his arm.

The crow dipped its head. With a lazy wing beat, it took to the air. But instead of landing on AJ's arm, it circled the attic, opening and closing its beak as if it was trying to caw an alarm.

"Fine," AJ said, "your funeral."

In five strides, he was at the hatch and away.

Meanwhile, Charlie circled higher, banging madly against the skylight. Outside, something cracked on the roof and rattled loudly down the slates. I tugged at my jacket but still couldn't rip it or work my arm free. By now, the first wisps of smoke were through the hatch, raising a light gray fug in the room. Again I heard something smack against the roof. At the same time, from the room downstairs came a billowing whumph of escalating flames, followed by a crash as something fell over. The smoke increased. Sweat beaded on my face, carrying the taste of fear into my mouth. I heard rafters splintering along the grain. In desperation, I looked around for anything I could use to cut my jacket, when

BANG! a stone came through the skylight, bringing down glistening shards of glass like fresh snow breaking off a winter branch.

My first thought was that it must be Mulrooney. Maybe he'd been in position on the roof, watching the conflict all the time. But that was dumb and I knew it. And so did Charlie. He fluttered out of sight as a hail of black objects rained through the skylight, and the attic filled with crows.

One of them was more than a crow.

"Freya!" I gasped as she materialized into human form. "How . . . ?"

"Bathroom window," she said, heaving at my jacket. "Had to break that one as well. Wouldn't worry about it. Don't think he'll be sending us a bill." She ran for a piece of glass.

Coughing, I said, "But I thought Preeve cured you?"

She slashed a hole in my sleeve. "Get real, Michael. You don't cure the dead. I was playing them until I could get out." She threw away the glass and tore at the fabric, calling the crows to help. The heat pressed in like a slow-moving wall, but at last the sleeve ripped and I was able to wriggle free.

But as the crows scattered and Freya helped me up, a belt of flame jumped through the hatch, preventing any means of reaching the fire escape.

I looked at the skylight. It was small and high, but our only chance. "The desk," I said. "We need to pull it over so I can stand on it."

She shook her head. "No time."

She was right. The flames had caught hold of some insulating material and were spreading fast, running along the eaves and licking up between the rafters. I'd be toast before I found my balance. "Okay," I panted, closing my eyes. "I'm going to try and —"

"No!" She grabbed my shoulders and shook me. "No reality shifts. You're dazed. You don't know what might happen. And I don't want it all changed again. I could lose you this time. I couldn't bear that, Michael."

Her eyes were filming.

"But I'll be dead if —"

"No. I know a way out. It will work, but you have to trust me."

With a snap, the frame of the hatch disappeared. Whatever she was planning, it had better be good. Frightened, I nodded.

"It takes a little sacrifice, that's all," she said. "Look at me. Remember me as I was. Dark hair, kinda scratchy. Pixie ears. Cute when you saw me from my best side. Don't ever forget I was Freya, not Devon."

"Freya, I don't understand what —?"

But by then she'd pulled aside my collar and sunk her teeth into the wound on my neck. I screamed in agony. For a second or two, my blood ran hotter than the attic. Then she gasped and stood away, wiping her mouth. "That's gonna look messy in the morning. Might take some explaining to your mom."

"What have you done?" I felt for my neck. It was raw with pain. My fingers were smeared with red-black blood.

She tottered backward and dropped to her knees.

"Freya, what have you *done?*" I screamed. I ran forward and caught her as she fell. The crows were flapping, cawing like crazy. All the while, the heat pressed in.

"Only way to set me free," she whispered. Her eyes glazed over, turning black.

"No!" I cried. "No, you can't die."

"Not dying," she croaked. "Changing. For good." She raised a hand and stroked my chest. Feathers were forming again on her skin.

"You mean —?"

"Fly," she breathed. "Believe and it will happen. Fly, Michael. I'll be waiting for you." She jerked and gave a shuddering caw. And right there in my arms, she turned into a crow and fluttered away, leading the others out through the roof.

Shaking, I brought my hand to my face. Glossy black feathers were growing out of my skin. "What have you done?" I whispered again. I stared at the open sky. *Come to me*, it seemed to be saying.

Come to me, Michael.

King of the crows.

30 · COWL

When I was young, we had all done it — "flown" off the peak of Begworth Tor. It needed a group of eight to make it safe. One to fly, the rest to do the catching. In turns we would run up the ramp of earth that made a shallow wave at the top of the hill, then dive off, arms wide, surfing the air, into the canopy of palms below. It was a short but exhilarating drop. In that second it took to be caught, if you were brave enough to raise your head, the horizon disappeared and, momentarily, until everyone collapsed in a heap of laughing bodies (and in Ryan's case, once, a broken wrist), you knew what it felt like to fly.

But it was nothing compared to what happened to me that morning in the burning remains of The Fourth Enchantment.

I felt the change in my upper body first. A sudden compression of the chest cavity, followed by a shift of strength to my shoulders. My legs retracted and my face reshaped. My fingers fused together in lines. And out of the natural tip they formed grew the fanlike feathers that marked a crow's wings.

The rest just happened by instinct. I snapped my wings open, beat down, and flew.

Takeoff was the hardest part. Even though I had no weight to speak of, the strength required to generate thrust made my wing joints ache. The fire was helpful in that respect. The air was swirling but always going up. By the third beat, I had raised myself high enough to make use of the mounting thermals. Near the skylight, I flapped again and caught a stray feather on a shard of glass still stuck in the frame. I cawed in pain. But the impetus was with me then and I powered through a shower of rising embers and up, up, up into the open sky.

Two crows immediately circled me, echoing their calls across my air space. They used no words, only rasps of noise. It was a language all the same. Mom had once told me I was a master of the early-morning grunt. She had never known anyone who could use the sound *umm* to mean so many different things, she said. I had the same experience now with the crows. The human ear only heard *caw!* or *cark!* (a sound frequently clipped to *ark!* by the crows). But there was more, much more, to their calls than that. I was able to detect subtle changes in tone, vibrancy, attack, duration and instinctively translate them into single words or simple phrases. *Me! You! Turn! Higher! She waits!*

"She" being Freya.

I called back: *I look!*

At least that's what I tried to say. One of the crows returned a doubtful *Ark?!*

I beveled my wings and circled lower. It was effortless. Wonderful. The heat from the fire continued to support me, but now I could stretch and glide with the currents, flicking my wing tips only for momentum or tilting them to alter course.

I swiveled one eye and looked down. The fire was in the middle of the run of buildings but not yet spreading to either side. The central part of the roof had collapsed and the air above the hole was choked with smoke and floating cinders, parted here and there by spikes of flame. A crowd had gathered in the service road. Were any of them UNICORNE agents, I wondered? Where had *they* been when Freya and I needed them? Where, indeed, were Mulrooney and Klimt?

She waits! the crows called again.

Ark! I cried. A terse but seemingly appropriate acknowledgment. Every sound they made was like a battle cry. There was nothing gentle about these birds.

I wheeled upward and let the air carry me back, following my escorts to a series of intersecting rooftops peppered with chimneys of differing heights. The entire flock was there, arranged along a row of ancient ridge tiles dabbed with parched and dying moss. They were in resting mode, necks short, breasts puffed, eyes blinking, bored. One of them was Charlie, taken prisoner, flanked by a pair of much larger crows, the type of bruisers who wouldn't think twice about pecking out an eye or tearing off a leg. Charlie did not look like a happy bird.

On a cowl on the tallest chimney sat Freya. It was difficult to say how I knew it was her. At first glance, every crow looked the same (though their sizes varied and some shone brighter in their feathers than others). It was her bearing, perhaps. Or the shape of her neck. Or the angle of her beak. Or simply the fact that no other crow was perched higher.

I landed awkwardly and was met by a ripple of derisory carks as I scrabbled onto a mortar flashing a foot below Freya's perch.

"Not there," she cawed, snapping out a warning to a pair of other males who were vying to join her on her throne.

My privilege, I guessed.

With a show of feathers that annoyed the bird next to me (*Ark!*) I fluttered up beside Freya and folded my wings.

"Be bold," she said, moving sideways to give me space. "They will drive you away if you show any sign of fear or weakness."

Rrrk! I grated, unable to twist the sentence I wanted out of my throat.

"Be patient. Speech will come," she said. "The words of the crow are harsh and direct. If you think I sound cold or blunt, that's simply a sign that your humanity is still intact. Listen well, Michael." She shook her neck as a gust of wind buffeted the chimney tops. Externally, I felt no cold. Inside, every hollow bone was rattling. "I gave you the crow curse to save your life. But I lost my grip on the old world with it. I can't turn back. I can never be the girl you knew. You can turn, but you must be wary. The curse is strong. It will claw at your soul. It will try to claim you. Sleep will be difficult. The only way to be rid of the spell is to do as I did to you. And if you should bite, Michael, bite hard. Anything less will kill you. Look down at the road now. What do you see?"

The white van. Alexander's van. Parked on a small gash of wasteland near the bus station. He was leaning against the hood, using binoculars to watch what was happening at the store. Two fire engines had just hosed up, all horns and flashing lights. Firefighters spilled from both the trucks and started herding the crowd away. Alexander, I noticed, was scanning the faces.

"He is looking for you," Freya said.

I dipped my head. "He is — *ark!*" No matter how I tried, I couldn't get my tongue around "He's the Bulldog's son." But none of that mystery mattered to her now.

"My crows are yours to command," she said. "They will kill him if you wish. Even with his powers, he could not stop us all."

"No," I croaked. "He has . . . words" — *information* was too hard to form — "I need. He must be tak-en."

"What do you want us to do?" she asked.

I looked at Charlie and had an idea. "Would A-lex know a-noth-er crow?"

She moved her head from side to side. Somewhat spitefully she said, "You want his 'pet' to return?"

"No, not . . ." — I couldn't find the shapes to say *Charlie* — "I will go. I will . . . fffol-low him. He will not know it is me."

Ark! she cried. A sound of approval. A war cry almost. She liked the idea. Most of the others echoed it back.

A bird on lookout gave a sharp call.

Alexander's van was moving.

Freya's dark eyes locked onto mine. "Go. Take what you need from him. But know this, Michael. He tried to kill me. He is our enemy. When you are done, you will give him to us."

Not a request, a no-nonsense order.

Ark! Ark! Ark! she called savagely. And she took off, rousting the others to flight.

I tried to jump with them. But in the clatter of wings and cross movements of air, I lost my bearings and slipped off the cowl, righting myself with a lumbering flap that made me smack one wing against the ridge. Painful. But not nearly as painful as what I saw in the gutter at the edge of the roof. A dying crow lay there, staring at the sky, a hole in its bleeding throat. It was Charlie, cruelly punished for his innocent allegiance to a crazy human. Silently, I said a prayer for him, then raced after the van, following it out of the town limits. As I chased Alexander down the roads, I wondered how much mercy Freya and her crows would show to him. The answer came back as cold as the spots of rain on my wings.

None. He was a dead man walking.

Not far out of town, well inland from the sea, the van turned into an industrial park. I watched it weave through the maze of buildings, right to the end, where it stopped out of sight beside a disused factory displaying a damaged sign: CORK- ETTE's CA PETS. Every window on the ground floor was boarded up, but as I circled overhead, I watched Alexander lift a loose panel, then climb inside and put the board back. I dropped down and landed on a higher sill where the windows were glazed but mostly broken. Taking care this time to pro- tect my wings, I hopped through a hole in the glass.

Despite the fact that I'd entered at a higher level, the fac- tory turned out to be just one floor high. A huge, empty sack of a place, big enough to hold a couple of small aircraft. There were large bleached spaces on the concrete floor — the ghosts of heavy machinery, long gone. Between the spaces were oily patches, bits of tarpaulin, and other junk. Cables hung loose from a framework of steel joists in the ceiling that supported a system of venting fans. Fixed to the wall in various places were access ladders that led to the roof. In one corner was a run-down office with a window that looked onto the factory floor. I could see a desk and a filing cabinet. An old calendar clung lopsided to the wall. There was a mattress on the floor and a camping stove, plus a few basic provisions. Next to the desk was a tall gray locker, stripped of its door. Hanging in the locker were two or three lab coats.

Alexander was sitting on an upturned crate with his back to the door. I watched him take my phone from his pocket. He weighed it in his hand for several moments, then tapped the screen and put it to his ear. I swooped down and landed silently on an oil drum, close enough to hear what he was saying.

"No, it's not Michael. Michael is . . . unavailable. Permanently unavailable. A nasty accident in The Fourth Enchantment. To whom do I have the displeasure of speaking? I'm afraid he's simply listed you as AK."

Ark! The cry just spilled right out of me — the shock of knowing he was talking to Klimt.

He looked sharply over his shoulder. He was surprised to see me, but I could tell from his reaction that he thought I was Charlie. So far, so good.

He stood up and headed out of the office. "What do I want? How about my father's head on a pole?" As he approached, he ran a knuckle down the side of my neck. I tried not to back away, but some lean was inevitable. Twenty minutes ago, this man had left me for dead in a fire. "Don't play games. You know who I am. I want the Bulldog here within the hour. You'll be tracing this call, so you'll know where to find me." He crooked a finger, inviting me onto his hand. For a moment, he raised me up and squinted at me, then put me onto his shoulder. Convenient. Now I could hear Klimt's voice.

The android said, "That is not possible."

"Of course it's *possible*," Alexander said, leaving some specks of spit on the phone. "This is UNICORNE. Anything is possible."

"And if we refuse?"

He gave a threatening laugh. "Then I'll be making an appointment to see my *doctor*. Strictly off hours, of course."

There was a pause. Klimt said, "Dr. Nolan played no part in your misfortune."

Dr. Nolan? What did he have to do with this? My claws curled tightly, finding muscle. *Stop that*, Alexander mouthed. He turned back to Klimt. "Is that what my father calls it? Misfortune?" His hand squeezed around the phone. "Mother would still be alive if it wasn't for Nolan."

"My version of events would not agree with that," said Klimt, in his usual precise and unflustered voice. "The evidence points to your acting alone. Your father had nothing to do with it."

Alexander began to pace. I was so close to his neck I could hear his teeth grinding. "He had everything to do with it. Everything! He brainwashed me from the age of four, long before I was part of your setup. He gave me the Tommies. He created the army. He . . . *billeted* the men here. *Here*, in my head." He tapped his temple. "My father taught me command was everything. *Stand down, Hodges! I'm dealing with this!* I wasn't a son; I was a weapon to be trained. Another UNICORNE *experiment*. As for Nolan, he let Mother slip. He could have saved her. Should have saved her."

"I am led to understand she was dead when the doctor arrived," said Klimt.

"Liar! Who *are* you?"

There was a pause, and then Klimt said chillingly, "We have photographs of what you did."

"What the *army* did! The *army!*" Alexander ranted. "It was what the men wanted. Payback for the Tommies. She shouldn't have put the dolls in the trash. I warned her NEVER to touch my things. *Get back in line, Grimper! I said, get back! Or you'll face a court-martial in the morning!*"

"Listen to me," Klimt said calmly. "Your army is out of control. It will soon become destructive and destroy your mind."

Alexander kicked an oil drum, sending a hollow boom around the walls.

"Give yourself up," said Klimt. "We can help you. Use what mental strength you possess to stand the army down and —"

"I want him here," Alexander snarled. "One hour, or I go after Nolan. And then I start talking — and you know what I mean. All about the DNA program. Trust me, I've got plenty to say to the world about you and your weird little alien *fish*. I assume the boy was your latest recruit? Stupid, sending him after me."

I turned full circle on Alexander's shoulder. My head was doing cartwheels. Twice now he'd mentioned a DNA program. I still had no idea what it meant, but I was sure it was linked to Dad somehow.

"Michael is extremely gifted," said Klimt. "I advise you not to underestimate him."

"Weren't you listening? The boy is dead. One hour. And don't try anything smart. If you send the Marine or the cute French girl, make sure you say your good-byes to them first."

And he ended the call by hurling the phone at a wall, dislodging me from his shoulder in the process.

"Charlie!" he barked after a moment's calm.

I was perched on a strut in the ceiling void, trying to decide what to do — if anything.

"Charlie!" he roared again. "Come on, boy. It's just you and me now. Come down. I've got some . . . treats for you."

He made a perch of his arm.

What could I do? If I changed into a boy again, he'd surely kill me. If I attacked him, the result might be the same. If I flew away, I would learn nothing.

He clicked his fingers.

So I spread my wings and glided down, scrabbling slightly for a hold on his arm.

"Steady, boy," he said, stroking my back. "Smoke got into your landing gear?" He walked me to the office desk and jerked open a drawer. Inside were some sticks of gum and a bag of peanuts. The bag was split and the nuts looked dried and old. He scooped up a handful and held them to my beak. "There you go, boy. Have a peanut."

I hadn't seen anything more unappetizing since Josie had tried to bake cereal cakes. I picked up a nut. Eating, I swiftly discovered, was as much a challenge as flying. I'd seen birds catch insects and work them backward into their mouths, but in practice it was hard to get the action right.

I dropped the nut.

"Oops." He presented his hand again.

I was less ambitious this time. I picked up a half nut and managed to get it into my throat. It felt like a small cannon-ball. I glugged as I tried to force it down.

"Careful," Alexander said. He opened his hand and let the rest of the peanuts spill. Then pinching my neck between his finger and thumb, he gently massaged the sides of my throat. "Now, here's a strange thing," he said. "Never knew my Charlie liked peanuts before. Unless, of course, you're not my Charlie . . ."

He pressed his fingers together, making me gag.

"And Charlie . . . doesn't . . . *squawk*."

He smirked and pressed harder.

By all the laws of physics, I should have been dead. Bizarrely, the peanut saved me. It was lodged so tightly, it prevented my puny neck from being crushed. At the same moment, I saw a movement behind Alexander, and a hand came down in a chopping motion at the back of his neck.

He groaned and dropped to his knees.

Hey-ho, the cavalry had come. In the shape of my favorite Marine.

Mulrooney.

You want life to be simple. But it never is. When Agent Mulrooney turned up, I thought I was clear of danger. I was wrong. Mulrooney was an experienced soldier. He knew how to hit a man to render him unconscious. Under normal conditions, he would have succeeded. But nothing about this conflict was normal. The one thing Mulrooney hadn't considered was the unexpected.

Me.

When Alexander closed his fingers around my neck and the threat of being choked grew real, I became human again. I fell to the floor and crashed against the locker, bringing down one of the lab coats and its hanger. I was gasping for air and semi-naked, my regular clothing lost somewhere in the transfer from boy to crow and back. All I had around me was one of those "shawls" I'd seen on Freya, clinging like an eggy membrane to my skin.

Mulrooney jolted in shock and caught Alexander with only a glancing blow. The Marine had just enough time to utter my name before Alexander said, "*Company*," and called on his army for help.

From a shelf on the wall above the desk, a spare can of gas for the camping stove flew across the room and struck Mulrooney on the temple. *Donk!* The sound rang out like a hammer on an anvil. Mulrooney staggered sideways. Alexander managed to rise and kick Mulrooney hard in the gut. The Marine spat out a frothy lump of phlegm and tumbled through the doorway, clutching his stomach. Alexander was slight of build, but the kick was effective. Mulrooney was seriously weakened. But instead of pursuing him and pressing his advantage, Alexander reached into the locker and selected one of the lab coats. He plucked a pair of boffin specs from the pocket, breathed on each lens, and put the specs on.

"I'll deal with you shortly, crow boy," he said. "*Clegg, watch him.*"

He stepped out onto the factory floor, making his threatening A-shaped stance. He liked posing, liked the theater of power. But it made him overconfident and Mulrooney knew it. I raised myself onto one elbow, in time to see Mulrooney's attempt to hit back. What looked like a scrap of metal winged through the air and buried itself in Alexander's neck. He squealed like a week-old puppy. Unsurprisingly, there was nothing cute about his response. "*Company!*" he screamed. I heard a coarse rattle and saw a hook speeding down from a pulley near the ceiling. It crashed into Mulrooney like a train colliding with a cow on the tracks, followed by fold after fold of chain. Mulrooney groaned, sank down, and went deathly quiet. Alexander swayed a little. The exertion of moving something that heavy had taken its toll. He tore the scrap of metal from his neck, saving his *arrgghh!* for the effort of throwing the spike aside. Panting angrily, he turned and staggered back into the office.

Where I was waiting.

I was on my feet, wearing one of the lab coats.

And the glasses I'd found in the pocket.

"What the —?" he snarled. "*Clegg! I told you to —*"

"*Company!*" I roared before he could finish. "*Company, stand down! Ignore all orders!*"

His eyes bulged behind his glasses. A drop of blood the size of a raisin dripped off his neck and started what would soon become a bigger stain on the collar of his lab coat. Mulrooney had injured him more seriously than I'd thought. The wound looked pretty bad. Alexander covered it again with his palm, this time keeping his hand in place. But however bad the pain or the loss of blood, it hadn't dented his sense of humor. He started to laugh, as though he couldn't quite believe what he'd heard me say. *Company, stand down? Ignore all orders?* What kind of upstart kid would mess with his army of faceless men?

He blinked and a coat hanger rose into the air. One of those plastic ones with a hook that screwed out. *"Hold it steady!"* he barked. Right before my eyes, he kept the hook in place but turned the arms, making the plastic spin so fast that it detached and flew away like a leaf hitting the spokes of a bicycle wheel.

"You're nothing," he breathed, turning the point of the hook toward me. "I admit, you can throw a few cheap surprises, better than the average Talen they find, but if you think —"

"I've seen them," I said.

His brow twitched.

"I've been in your head. I've talked to the men. They don't want you in command anymore. They want me."

He laughed again, but there were serious flecks of confusion in his eyes.

I made the A stance. "Clegg was supposed to be guarding me. But he let me get up. He's shifted sides."

"Oh, yeah?" Alexander said. The hook flew at me, the screw thread coming for the center of my forehead. But a hairsbreadth from the point of contact, it stopped and performed a jittery turn, like the second hand of a watch when the battery is running down. *"Engage!"* Alexander screamed. He blinked in fury, but all that moved were the beads of sweat on his furrowed brow.

"Dobbs, stand down," I said calmly.

I could almost visualize the soldier, like a vapor trail wafting behind a thin veil. His hand unsteady on the curve of the hook. His eye lines flicking up and down, unsure.

Alexander shook with rage. Blood seeped out between his fingers like cream from a squeezed profiterole. *"Dobbs, you mangy, cowardly swine! Grimper, take over! Grimper! Engage!"*

The hook fell to the floor.

"They're deserting you," I said. "Clegg's spread the word. Payback for the doll you left in the store."

"Tommy," he gasped, his eyes popping. "He was on the countertop. I forgot to take him."

"You're under arrest," I said. "I'm taking you in for interrogation. You're going to tell me everything you know about my father."

No, not Tommy, he mouthed, almost visibly crumpling. He lifted his hand away from his neck. I thought for a moment he would launch himself at me (I was clutching a screwdriver in my pocket, expecting it). Instead, he gave a crestfallen salute and staggered away. Before I realized what was happening, he'd stepped out of the office and closed the door. I flung myself at the handle. Too late. A key turned in the lock.

"Alexander!" I hammered the door. There was a window panel in it, strengthened by cross wires. No way was I going to break through. I ditched the boffin specs and pressed my face to the glass. He walked past the chains that had fallen on Mulrooney and started to climb one of the ladders toward the roof. "Alexander!" I screamed again. "Stop!" I had no idea what he intended to do or whether he was simply planning to escape, but at that moment I saw Chantelle on the factory floor, aiming her laser device at him.

"Noooooooo!" I screamed as a blue light streaked through the air and struck Alexander between the shoulders. He fell off the ladder like a folding flag. And all I could think as I watched him drop was *Where are the men when I need to command them?*

What had happened to Alexander's Army?

I was still kicking the door when Chantelle opened it. "Calm down, it is over," she said. "What is with the white coat? Are you hurt?"

I sprinted past her and ran to Alexander.

"Malone, I need you here!" she shouted. She had moved to Mulrooney and was on her knees, starting to drag the heavy chains off him. But I'd looked at Mulrooney and seen him breathing; he was going to be all right. The same could not be said of Alexander. He lay motionless on his back, a blood pool billowing around his head.

I skidded to my knees and pulled the boffin glasses off him. "Alexander, hold on." I gripped his shoulders, feeling the warmth of the blood he was leaking. Chantelle's laser had immobilized him, but his lips were still moving slightly. "Alexander." I shook him gently. His eyes were half-closed, like an old man falling asleep on a sofa. "UNICORNE is coming. They're going to take care of you." I could hear the sound of vehicles pulling up outside. "Tell me about my father, please."

"Dayton," he muttered. "Chief sci . . . officer. 41625."

"Please!" I shook him again. "It's Michael. What's the DNA program?"

"Deen-A," he said, grinning like a cartoon cat. "Wheeeeeee!"

A loud cracking noise made me look over my shoulder. One of the window panels was being removed by a crowbar. Two men I'd never seen before were coming through the window space Alexander had used to gain entry. They were wearing the pale orange uniform of UNICORNE. One had a medical bag slung across his shoulder. "Here!" Chantelle called. The man with the bag ran directly to her. The other took a good look at Alexander. Seeing no danger, he nodded at me once and hurried over to help Chantelle.

I tried Alexander one more time, quoting the message I'd found in Dad's study. "*In New Mexico: Dragons abound.* Do you know what it means?"

"41625 Dayton . . ." he said. "Alexander Jon . . ." Then he groaned and passed out.

By now, agents were pouring in like ants through a door crack. One of them lifted me clear of Alexander.

"You all right, sir?" he whispered, as if it was me running the op.

"Where's Klimt?" I growled.

"Sir, you look hurt. Should I call —?"

"WHERE'S KLIMT?!" I raged, and batted him away.

"All right, I'll deal with this." Chantelle ranged up. She gestured the man aside, grabbed me by the shoulders, and turned me to face her. "Where's the girl? Where's Freya?"

"What do you care? Where were *you* when we needed you? Buying shoes in the mall?"

She slapped my face. "I told you, you need to calm down."

But I went for her instead, only to find myself looking at a red light blinking in the screen at the front of her device. The man who'd tried to help me fingered his collar. Another man gestured to him not to interfere.

"The weapon is set to maximum," she said, purring through her soft French accent. "Unlike him, you might never wake up." She gestured at Alexander. "Klimt's orders were very clear. I am to stop you both if necessary. Now, *where* is Freya?"

"Dead!" I lied. "Dead in the fire you let her burn in."

Her cold brown eyes showed no remorse. "How did you escape?"

I looked at Mulrooney. He was lying on a stretcher, holding an oxygen mask to his face. There was no point trying to conceal the truth. He'd seen what he'd seen. Klimt and the Bulldog would soon know it, too. "I flew out through the skylight," I said. And before she could crease her manicured eyebrows, I morphed into a crow and took off through one of the unboarded windows.

Outside, Freya and the other crows were waiting, lining the roof of the factory opposite.

"Well?" she carked as I came in to land.

"They have him," I replied.

"You promised him to *us*."

"I know, but —"

Ark! went a brute of a crow beside her. Several feathers were missing on its forehead, and one of its claws had been eaten by disease. It tipped its beak, wanting us to look at something on the ground. Chantelle had stepped out of the factory, looking around to see where I'd gone. She spotted the row of birds and said something to one of the agents, the same one who'd tried to help me in the factory. He opened a breast pocket and passed her a pair of binoculars. The crows chattered and paddled their feet as she panned the binoculars along the line.

Unfazed, Freya said, "Did he tell you what you needed to learn?"

"No."

"Too bad," she said, with venom in her throat. She rippled her neck, making the feathers there stiffen and lift. Right and left of me, birds were getting ready to strike.

"You can't at-tack," I warned her. (I was still having trouble with multisyllable words.) "You'll die. Like the crows on the cliff."

Her dark eyes tilted a few degrees downward.

"I told them you were dead. If you leave, you'll be safe."

Ark! she went. An angry, life-affirming battle cry that all the crows repeated back to her.

"It makes sense, don't you see? It means you can be free."

Ark! they grated. *Ark! Ark! Ark!*

"Leave!" I carked back as fiercely as I could, rocking my body to reinforce the statement. "Your foe is down. His men are gone. What is the point of dying now?"

"Honor," croaked Freya.

Ark! I sneered, inviting the glare of the guardian brute who clearly had a bit of a thing for her.

She fanned her tail, and the cries faded out. The brute reluctantly backed down. "Speak," she said.

I met her eye. "You saved me so I could be with you. Would you fly to your death and leave me so soon? All for the sake of a man de-feat-ed?"

Ark, she grated. More of a grizzle than a cry this time. "Where are his men?"

"Gone," I repeated. "His mind is bro-ken."

She jerked her head and looked straight down. A black car had just sluiced up. A door clicked open and Amadeus

Klimt stepped out, pulling his jacket cuffs straight. He exchanged a word or two with Chantelle. She offered him the binoculars. He refused them, but rolled his gaze over the rooftop anyway.

The birds began to shuffle impatiently. To stare at a crow was to make a threat. And no one stared better than Amadeus Klimt.

Freya widened her beak and gave a sudden command. *Ark-Ark!*

There was hesitation. A twitching exchange of glances. *Ark?* went the brute.

Ark-ARK! Freya screamed.

And just as if they'd seen a fox coming, every other bird except the two of us scattered.

Klimt continued to hold his gaze.

My breast puffed up with fear. "Why did you do that? Now he knows it's us. If he thinks you're alive, he'll come for you again."

A wisp of air flew in through Freya's nostrils, the crow equivalent of a human snort. She put her face to the wind, feeling it keenly. "Crows do not fear death or conflict. I do not care what Klimt knows." She spread her wings to their maximum extent. "Alexander is yours. Go back to them, Michael. You have unresolved business."

"What do you mean?"

"You are wrong about the army. The men are not gone. They are close. I sense them."

"Close?" I queried.

"To you," she said. "Look for me when you need a friend." And she sank through the air toward Klimt. Less than six feet from him, she banked and disappeared into the distance. He smiled thinly. Not once had he flinched.

Now it was me and him. He laced his fingers. I shivered in the wind. In the background, UNICORNE agents stretchered Alexander out of the factory and loaded him into a private ambulance. One of them closed the ambulance door and banged it to signal it was okay to leave. I glanced at the ambulance driver. His window was open, his forearm resting on the car door. He was doing something with his hand, tumbling a coin across his knuckles, a trick Dad used to do at birthday parties, though I was sure I'd seen someone else do it recently. The ambulance pulled away. Klimt gave me another extended look, then turned and got into his car. A signal to say he had drawn a line between us. Capturing Alexander was his victory, not mine. So, like Freya, I spread my wings and flew away, sailing on the wind toward the coast and the one shred of hope I had left — a row of four cottages that overlooked the sea on Berry Head West, one of which was home to my father's doctor.

The ever-mysterious Liam Nolan.

As the sea loomed closer, so did the rain — which was a blessing, in part. The cold ping of water slowed my impulsiveness and straightened out my thinking. There was no point going to Liam now. At this time of day, he was probably working. And if I did confront him, I'd be unclothed again. And I could hardly tap on his office window and hope he understood crow.

So I changed course and flew over Holton, following the landmarks that would take me home. I landed in the backyard, scaring off a bunch of chattering sparrows. Praying that Mom hadn't come home for lunch, I quickly changed into my human form, got rid of the shawl, and lifted the plant pot that hid the spare key. I bolted upstairs and into the shower. The water was warm and comforting. The only reminders of my morning "adventures" were the sting when the heat hit the wound on my neck and the sight of blood swirling into the drain. I remembered Freya saying, *That's gonna look messy.* She wasn't wrong. I nearly died when I checked the bathroom mirror. The bite marks were grue-some. Mom would go ape if she saw them. I washed the wound as best I could and found a bigger bandage to cover it with. If Mom asked, I would tell her I'd scratched and made it worse. Picking at scabs was a standard boy thing. Every mother knew that.

I spent the afternoon sweating over a laptop in Josie's room. I had zero interest in my sister's surroundings, but her window had the very best view of the driveway. I wanted to be ready if Klimt came knocking. I even opened a small window in case I needed to fly.

I typed Dad's message into a search engine. *In New Mexico: Dragons abound.* A lot of useless stuff came back, mostly to do with tourism or weather, along with a bunch of hits about dragon books and dragonflies. The images were better. The New Mexico landscape looked pretty alien, the perfect place for a UNICORNE mystery. It was mostly desert, filled with scrubby plants and solemn tabletop moun-tains called mesas. One image made me catch my breath — a border sign saying WELCOME TO NEW MEXICO, LAND OF ENCHANTMENT. I spent AGES on that, hoping to find some connection to Alexander or The Fourth Enchantment. But none of the searches gave me any clues. It was the same when I put in *DNA program.* That brought up tons of chemistry sites and images of something called an alpha-helix. On a learning scale, it was a better school day than a regular one, but I was getting nowhere with solving the message.

The only search I had any success with was on the word *artifact*. I remembered Freya saying she'd heard Klimt or Preeve use the term several times. The search engine came back with two possible dictionary definitions:

1. An object made by a human being, typically one of cultural or historical interest

2. Something observed in a scientific investigation or experiment that is not naturally present but occurs as a result of the preparative or investigative procedure

Both definitions got me thinking, particularly the second one, which sounded very "UNICORNE." But by four p.m., when Mom's car turned into the drive, I hadn't worked anything out. So I shut the laptop and took it downstairs, putting it on the table where it usually sat. One of the first things Josie did when she was home from school was to log in to a chat room she shared with her friends. Like they didn't have enough to blab about all day? Sure enough, she hit the computer as soon as she was in (sparing a moment to stick out a pimple of tongue at me).

"Hello, love. Good day?" Mom came in, unraveling a scarf.

"Umm," I grunted. I could hardly tell her I'd almost died in a fire and now had a very slight taste for worms. A grunt was just about the safest response.

She spotted the bandage right away. "What's happened to your neck?" A slight squeak of alarm/annoyance/*do we need to jab you for tetanus?* creeped into the end of the sentence.

Josie glanced my way and sniffed. "It would be so much cooler if he left the bolts showing. Ha, ha."

I told Mom the scratching lie; she bought it whole.

"Honestly, I should put you in mittens," she muttered.

"Pink ones," said Josie.

"And why have you changed your sweater?"

Oops. I'd forgotten about the clothes. It was always the simple things Mom noticed, the things I tended to forget. The clothes I'd gone out in were probably still being hosed by the fire brigade. The jeans, thankfully, were pretty standard; I had several pairs of look-alike denim. But the sweater . . . "I got cold," I said.

Feeble, but again she went for it.

"It's about time that old one went anyway. I'm forever mending holes in the sleeves. Leave it out; I'll drop it into a charity thrift shop."

"I can do that!"

Bad move. I'd piped up far too quickly. Now she was nursing a suspicious frown. I shrugged it off. "I'm going into Holton tomorrow."

She canceled the frown and did a double take. "Good grief. Did you hear that, Josie? Aliens have abducted my darling son and replaced him with an improved errand-running replica."

"In your dreams," Josie said.

I smiled cheesily and changed the subject. "What's for dinner?"

"See?" Josie said. "Hasn't changed a bit. Same old boring, predictable Mi . . . chael."

I spotted it, and so did Mom — the change in Josie's voice as she spoke my name. "You all right?" Mom asked.

Josie clicked her tongue, her quick eyes darting over the screen. "Just one of those stupid browser updates. I can deal with it."

"I'm sure you can," Mom said. "Lasagna, to answer your question, Michael. Forty minutes," she added as I headed for the stairs. "Josie, when you're done, go and get changed, please."

"Umm," she grunted.

Mom shook her head in despair. "Honestly, I could

swap you pair for a couple of chimps and not notice the difference."

"Umm," we went.

"Give me strength," Mom sighed, and went into the kitchen.

It must have been less than two minutes later that Josie walked into my room. She closed the door and sat down rigidly on my bed. She had that seriously pale look on her face, feet crossed at the ankles, hands in her lap. She tucked her hair behind her ears.

Something wasn't right.

I tried a mild caution. "Hel-lo? There's a sign on the door. You're supposed to knock before you —"

"Why were you looking up New Mexico on the computer?"

I'd forgotten to clear my search history. *Shoot.*

I turned my back so she couldn't see my face and pretended to sort some homework on my desk. "It's boring being suspended for two days. You start to think about all sorts of stuff. Dad was in my head, that's all."

"What does *DNA program* mean?"

My gut tightened. This was going to be worse than I'd thought. Josie had a bigger bite on her than Freya. Once she got her teeth into something, the Sherlock in her didn't let go. "Nothing. I was just messing with a search engine and —"

"*In New Mexico: Dragons abound*. That's not messing. That's very specific. What's going on, Michael? Why would you search on something like that? Tell me the truth or I'm going to show Mom."

A spy, I realized, would probably have to tie her up and gag her now. But however appealing that might have seemed, she was my sister and I loved her — and we both loved Dad.

Crisis point.

No escape.

She had to know the truth.

I turned to face her. "I found it scribbled on a slip of paper — in Dad's room."

Her pretty face shook. She didn't speak, or blink, for a whole five seconds. "Where?"

"Behind the picture of the tree."

"*Behind* it?"

"In an envelope taped to the frame."

"Why were you looking?"

"The picture was . . . tilted. I was trying to straighten it when the envelope dropped on the desk."

"And the message was in it?"

"Yes."

"In dad's handwriting?"

Interesting point. I hadn't thought about that. It would be easy to check, though. Mom had tons of letters and postcards from him. "Um, I guess."

"Let me see it."

I hesitated slightly and opened my desk drawer. I pulled the slip of paper out of the envelope, careful not to show her the initials.

She read it as though it had come from the president. "Why would he write this?"

"I don't know. I was trying to find out."

Her gaze drifted into the middle distance.

"Jose, this has to be our secret. You can't tell Mom. She'll get upset."

Josie chewed her lip. She looked pretty close to tears herself. "But what does it *mean*? Dragons?"

I raised my shoulders. In that respect, I was no wiser than she was.

She shuffled to the edge of the bed. "Have you looked in his room for any more clues?"

"No." I took the message back.

She gave a determined nod. "Okay. If I find anything, I'll let you know."

"Josie, you —"

No good. She was gone. I sighed and buried my face in my hands. Now I'd done it. The search for my father was about to enter a whole new chapter. The best brain in Holton was on the case. Josie Malone versus Amadeus Klimt.

And only a fool would bet against my sister.

Early next morning, Mom took Josie to her drama lesson. As soon as they were gone, I wheeled my bike out of the garage and set off for the coast. I had one real chance of finding Liam Nolan, one that didn't involve knocking on his house door or giving him a permanent fear of crows. I knew from my previous encounters with the family that on Saturday mornings, he walked their dog, Trace, along the Berry Head cliffs. It seemed a hopeless venture, but I had to try. I had to know his real connection to Dad.

I was lucky. Within minutes of reaching the cliff path, I saw him. He was tall, what Mom would call a sturdy man, with short reddish hair and a stylish gray beard that shaded the lower half of his face. He was strolling along looking out to sea as if he was seeking inspiration for a poem. He was wearing a waterproof coat, the kind with the waxy finish that Josie couldn't bear to touch. Trace's leash was spilling out of one pocket.

It was the dog who saw me first. She was sweeping the headland, sniffing at rabbit holes. As I drew near to them, she caught my scent. She stared, ears pricked, the way dogs do. I crouched lower in the saddle and cycled to her.

"Hey, Trace."

She jumped up, beating her paws against my thigh. She was the most fantastic dog, a gray-white husky with stunning blue eyes. I let her nuzzle my hand as Liam approached.

"Michael," he acknowledged me dourly, still preferring to aim his gaze at the water. He had a brown scarf bunched around his throat. His oval-shaped head looked exactly like an egg balanced upright on a nest.

"Hello, Dr. Nolan. I was just cycling up here and —"

"No, you weren't. I've walked this cliff path hundreds of times and never seen you here at this hour of the morning. What do you want?"

Brusque and to the point. But I could also be like that.

"To talk about my dad. He was your patient, wasn't he?"

"Get down," he said to Trace. He found the leash and clipped it to her collar, his coat panels crackling as he stretched his body over her. "Everything between a doctor and their patient is confidential. You're wasting your time."

"What about a doctor and his friend — or fellow agent?"

He sighed and crouched beside the dog, running his hand down each of her legs as if he were frisking her for hidden weapons. As he stood up, he took a smartphone from his pocket. "I have no idea what you're talking about."

"You work for UNICORNE. That makes us equals."

He glanced at the phone, tapped the screen a few times, and put it away. "You're deluded, Michael. Go home. I can't help you." He shook the chain to make Trace walk.

No way was I giving up that easily. I hauled the bike around and freewheeled after him. Above us, a seagull scythed across the sky. "I've seen you there. Klimt told me you work for them."

"I work privately for several clients. What of it?"

I swerved the bike to a stop in front of him, nearly running over his toes.

"What the Dickens do you think you're doing, boy?!" He was furious now.

"Not clients like them. I called your office and left you a message. Why didn't you respond?" I had checked my phone repeatedly before Alexander took it. Definitely no voice mails from Liam or his secretary.

"It may have escaped your attention," he snapped, his face reddening around the fringes of his beard, "but I'm a doctor. I have sick people to deal with. They take greater priority than children with overactive imaginations."

Oh, yeah? I ripped the envelope from my jacket and made

him look at it. "*LN*. That's you, isn't it? Liam Nolan. My dad wrote this. It was in his room."

"Yes, and every year Rafferty wrote a letter to Santa. What's your point, Michael?"

"'In New Mexico: Dragons abound.' That's the message he left for you. What does it mean?"

"I have no idea."

"You're lying."

"I *beg* your pardon!"

"I can read your eyes, like Dad could. Gold for truth. Green for lies. You're full of green flecks, Dr. Nolan."

That rattled him. Really rattled him. He leaned away as if I were some kind of monster. A fury of confusion was building in his face, when the phone beeped suddenly in his pocket. He fumbled his hand inside and retrieved it. He read the message slowly and put the phone back.

"Klimt?" I suggested. I was expecting his car to turn up at any moment, and was ready to fly away if I had to. It wouldn't have surprised me if Liam had tipped them off.

He looked along the headland. It was pretty much deserted. "Aileen hasn't been well," he said quietly, "ever since the business with the girl."

Aileen. His wife. Rafferty's mother. She'd been traumatized by everything that had happened with Freya. I caught a glimpse of his eyes again. Gold.

He breathed in deeply and composed himself, finding a moment to pat Trace's head. I thought this was it, that I'd broken him at last. Instead, he swallowed hard and stared at my bandage. "What's going on with your neck?"

"You know what happened. You were there when I recovered after Freya's attack."

"Freya?" he queried. Again, his flecks were gold. Either he was good at disguising a lie or he really didn't know what had happened to Freya.

"You treated me."

"For an infection, yes. The cause of the wound was never revealed to me. Perhaps you want to shed some light on that? You mentioned . . . Miss Zielinski? How could she possibly be involved?"

"Doesn't matter," I said.

"I think it does. The infection has progressed. I can see lesions developing and there is significant swelling in the surrounding tissues. You could die if that's not attended to. Take the bandage off. Here, I'll do it."

I batted him away. "First you tell me about my father." I grabbed the bike by its handlebars and thumped the front wheel down on the path.

Trace grizzled, not sure if she should growl or not. Liam shook the leash again and made her sit. "Don't make a scene," he said. "You know I can't give up UNICORNE secrets.

They tell me nothing, anyway." He looked along the headland again. The nearest people to us were miles away, attempting, unsuccessfully, to fly a kite.

"But you know *something*, don't you? About the DNA program. What is it? And why do they keep on telling me this lie about Dad going off looking for dragons?"

"I don't know!" he snapped. "As far as I'm aware, dragons only appear in children's books or the minds of new age fantasists. I am a doctor. I deal in rational truths. My job is to attend to the sick. They recruited me to help your father and have paid me a retainer ever since."

"UNICORNE?"

"No, Buckingham Palace! Of course I mean UNICORNE. That's what this silly interrogation is about, isn't it?"

"Help Dad? How?"

He muttered something under his breath. "They were experimenting with a breathable fluid, water supersaturated with a previously unstable isotope of oxygen. Once immersed, a human subject could experience enhanced powers of thought, well beyond modern computational levels."

"And Dad . . . tried this?"

"Your father was their primary study. Through him they achieved the neurological breakthrough that eventually led to the development of Klimt."

"So he did build Klimt," I gasped.

Liam looked across the water. "I'm led to understand that your father's input was greater than anyone's. That's all I know."

"What about you? What was your role?"

"Purely medical. It was my job to stabilize your father's body when . . ."

"When what?"

He took a long breath. The phone beeped again. This time he ignored it, but it seemed to make him anxious. "When his mind was elsewhere. Now will you let me look at that wound?"

I didn't know what to say. Dad's mind could leave his *body*? Was this the same thing I could do? What if Dad had been captured by a force like Alexander's Army — and somehow not gotten back?

"Lay your bike on the grass," Dr. Nolan said. "Brace yourself, this is going to hurt."

And he'd ripped away the bandage before I knew it.

The pain bent me double. By the time I could stand fully upright again, he was tilting a small bottle against a cotton pad. In the bottle was a clear, fruity-smelling liquid that made my nose twitch.

"What's that?"

"Alcohol to clean the wound. This place is prone to ticks. I carry it in case I have to remove one from the dog's legs.

Precautionary health measures go hand in hand with being a doctor, Michael. Look away. This is going to hurt."

I stretched my neck so he could see the wound properly. "I still don't understand Dad's message. Why would he leave you a note about dragons?"

"Don't talk." His breathing was a little unsteady.

But I *needed* to talk. This was the closest I'd been to the truth. "Could it be some kind of secret code?"

He pressed the cloth on and held it in place.

"Ow, that stings," I muttered.

"Not for long," he said, with a hint of regret. "Forgive me, Michael. I have to do this. There are greater forces at work here than me."

Even before he'd finished the sentence, the sea and the sky were changing places. Whatever he'd dispensed on that piece of cotton, it wasn't alcohol. I rocked sideways and sank into his arms. No time to fight, shift reality, or fly. All I could think of was that dumb idea that counting sheep helped you get to sleep. I had a new take on it. Counting huskies. I managed two from the dozens that had appeared like ghosts behind Trace.

And then I passed out.

I woke in the cube, in Preeve's laboratory, breathing the same mauve gas I'd seen Freya immersed in. My clothes had been replaced with a one-piece robe. The wound on my neck had been sealed without stitches. It was bare, but not painful. I seemed to have lost the instinct to fly. It would have been pointless, anyway. There was no deflection in the walls of the cube and no means of rocking it in any direction. I was still searching for a way out when Klimt walked into the lab with Preeve.

"Hello, Michael," said the android my father helped to build. "It appears we have a lot of catching up to do."

"Go to hell," I said.

"I very much doubt it exists. Not in the way most people imagine it."

"I know about you, Klimt. Liam told me things, about the experiments. What you did to Dad."

"What *we* did?" Preeve snorted, dropping his glasses to read a monitor. "Your father devised the whole DNA program. He was its most willing participant."

"What is it? What does DNA mean?"

Klimt sat on a stool directly in front of me while Preeve continued to browse around the lab, pecking at various pieces of equipment like a fish nipping weeds off the wall of its tank. "It is an acronym, Michael. Direct Neural Acceleration. It has a good ring to it, don't you think?"

I glanced at Preeve. He was shaking his head and tapping something into a tablet computer. He seemed to think this was all a big joke. "It makes your mind leave your body, doesn't it? Like what you do with the pulse down the phone."

Klimt straightened a crease in his trousers. "An elementary description, but to some degree accurate. Accelerating the power of thought has a profound effect on the individual's . . . perception of the universe, not unlike one of your reality shifts — which brings me to the primary reason I am here."

"I want to know about DAD!" I shouted.

"Doctor?" Klimt sighed.

Preeve came over and moved a knob on a freestanding control panel. Puffs of pale green gas squirted out of a line of pinprick vents in the floor of the cube, turning the mauve a slight shade of brown. The gas pressed into my lungs, making my head feel light. I sank to my knees, coughing. "Steady," said Klimt. "I want him to talk."

"He's already at a hyperbaric level," said Preeve. "We could just —"

"No." Klimt leveled a hand. "Nothing artificial. Not while his body is undergoing healing."

"It doesn't work," I panted.

"On Freya, no," he admitted. "I have to give the girl credit; she is far more cunning than I ever imagined. I hope you parted on agreeable terms. It may be a while before you see her again." He steepled his fingers and stared at the tips. "The treatment *will* nullify the virus in you. Unlike Freya, you are still human. I am afraid you have taken your last flight, however. It would have been interesting to monitor your newfound talent, but we could hardly send you home and let your mother face the trauma of watching the virus slowly take over. It would have happened at some point, trust me."

"How long are you keeping me here?"

"Till tomorrow at least," Preeve muttered.

"Are you crazy? Mom will call the police if —"

"Michael," Klimt cut in. He put his fingers through a little push-up routine. "You should know by now we have means of controlling your . . . domestic situation. You have been here for two days already."

"You're a monster."

He tilted his head. "Really? In comparison to whom? Preeve? Chantelle? You, perhaps?"

"Me? What have *I* done?"

"That is what I am here to find out. Chantelle tells me you were locked in an office during your conflict with Alexander. Did you attempt to control him with a reality shift?"

"No."

"Are you certain? Please think carefully. You were under great emotional stress. This is the time your shifts usually happen."

I threw up my hands. "Why are you asking me this? Has something changed?" One of the side effects of my shifts was that whenever I "reshuffled the multiverse" (one of Klimt's favorite descriptions of it) any trailing thoughts in my mind somehow got sucked into the altered reality. Josie, for instance, had gone from being completely nonmusical to a star flute player during one of my shifts, simply because I'd heard her make up a lie about taking flute lessons.

"Tell me precisely what happened," said Klimt.

I sighed and dragged my hands down my face. "He was climbing a ladder up to the roof. I was yelling at him to stop because he said he knew stuff about Dad. I was thinking about a shift, but then Chantelle came in and used that . . . laser thing on him. Where is he? I want to speak to him."

"Unfortunately, that will not be possible."

I looked into Klimt's motionless purple eyes.

"Alexander died in the ambulance," he said.

"He died?" I repeated, dry-mouthed with shock. "How?"

"I was hoping you might tell me. Did you kill him, Michael? Did you imagine a universe where Alexander died of his injuries?"

"No! Why would I do that? I told you, he knew about Dad — and UNICORNE. He said he was the Bulldog's son."

"Yes. A black day for the director, just one of the reasons I need to be clear about your . . . role in this."

"*My* role? You knew, didn't you? You and the Bulldog. I saw the way he looked at the Boffin cards. He sent me against his own son to see what would happen. Why?"

"Because no other Talen could have mastered Alexander. We needed you to bring him under control. If what you're telling me is true, you almost succeeded."

"I *didn't* harm him. Why would I lie?"

"Chantelle says you were wearing a laboratory coat. Why?"

"That was . . . I . . ."

"Why, Michael?"

"I . . . wanted to confuse him! To get my own back. He was losing them. The men. They wanted to desert. I saw them when I went out of my body."

"Saw them?" Preeve looked up from his tablet. "That's not possible, is it?"

Klimt said, "Please continue, Michael."

"I was trying to make them come over to me, but . . ."

"But what?"

"Maybe I *did* cause a shift? I remember being really angry and thinking, where were the men when I needed them?"

"Where indeed," said Klimt. He slowly got off the stool. "Keep him stable. I need to see the director."

"Klimt, wait!" I cried. "I didn't do anything. I swear, I wanted Alexander alive."

"Yes," he said, "I believe you, Michael. But if you did perform a reality shift around your thoughts of Alexander's Army, we have to accept the very real possibility that his men still exist as a functioning force."

"Outside his *mind*?" I glanced at Preeve again. His face was drawn into an anxious frown.

"You forget, this is UNICORNE. The extraordinary is merely ordinary to us."

"So . . . where are they — the men?"

I saw Klimt glance at a monitor that seemed to be displaying my brainwave patterns. "That, I do not know," he said. And he exited the lab, leaving me in the less than welcome company of Preeve.

"Right," said the scientist, nervously smoothing his hair off his brow. "We can do this one of two ways. I can make you sleep while the gas does its work or you can sit and study your fingernails. Either way, we're not going to talk. I certainly won't be pestered with ridiculous questions about the DNA program or your father's disappear —"

He stopped speaking as the door opened and two men I vaguely recognized walked in. One might have been the man who'd tried to help me in the factory. The other was carrying a medical bag. Both of them were wearing the pale-orange uniform.

"Yes, what is it?" Preeve said irritably. "Do you two even have access rights here?"

"Mr. Klimt sent us," the medic one said. He had a weird, clipped voice. He reminded me of someone.

Preeve grunted and went back to his tablet. "Well . . . be quick, whatever it is."

"We won't bovver you fer long," the first man said.

And the medic pulled a cotton pad out of his bag and held it across Preeve's nose and mouth. The scientist squeaked and dropped the tablet. He kicked three times, each kick fainter than the previous one, before sliding into a heap on the floor.

"What are you doing?" I gasped. "Wh-who are you?"

They stood at attention and clicked their heels.

"Private Clegg. *Sir!*"

"Private Hodges. *Sir!*"

They both saluted. And the faces I'd thought vague and forgettable briefly became terrifyingly plain. Two lines for eyes, one each for nose and mouth.

My question was answered. They were here, in the room.

Alexander's Army.

Made human.

Made men.

Clegg, the nonmedic, bent down and picked up the tablet computer. It seemed to puzzle him for a second, in the same way a caveman might wonder about a lightbulb he'd found in his cave. Then the eye slits burned with a faint mauve light, and the light scanned the screen from top to bottom. The keyboard came up. Clegg's fingers moved across it. With a hiss of compressed air, the gas around me disappeared and the cube lowered itself to the floor. All six walls dissolved in a shimmer, leaving a slightly raised platform marked along its edges by a faint yellow light.

Hodges held out my clothes. His face was human, yet strangely featureless. The sort of face that could have drifted into any situation and not be noticed or easily recalled.

"What do you want?" I said in a low-pitched tremor.

"Come to get you out, sir. You'll be needin' yer duds." He offered up the clothes again.

"No," I said weakly, gripping my arms as if I'd stepped out of a cold shower.

"Sir, you'll need yer duds up top," repeated Hodges.

"Operation Mother. It's a go," said Clegg. "Grimper 'n' Dobbs are waitin', sir. All we need is our orders to proceed."

"Mother?" I said, terrified that they meant mine. Their faces flickered between human and soldier. "The gas," I said quickly. "It fuddles your brain. Makes you forget things — mission details."

Clegg's features relaxed back to human. "We take the Bulldog, sir. Put you in 'is place. Run the joint our way. Payback — fer Mother."

So despite the fact I had given them form, Alexander's desire for revenge was still ingrained in their collective consciousness, driving them to complete his mission like a bomb counting down to detonation — a detonation only I might stop. "And then?"

"Then we learn the truth, sir. All about UNICORNE."

Which would have to include everything about Dad.

And suddenly, the mission didn't seem so crazy. A huge portion of my mind was screaming, *This is reckless! Pull out now!* I was a UNICORNE agent. I had a duty to raise the alarm. But when I thought about the lies that Klimt had told me and the danger he'd placed me in at the store, my quest for the truth began to tip me in favor of the army. Here was the chance I'd been waiting for.

I gave a minimal nod.

"Sir!" They both saluted again.

I took the clothes. While I changed, the men bound Preeve's wrists and ankles and stuck a piece of duct tape over his mouth. They dragged him onto the cube platform. Clegg picked up the tablet and re-formed the walls. The cube rose with Preeve inside. "Do you want 'im done for, sir?" Clegg's finger hovered over the keyboard.

"No," I said. "He could be useful to us later."

"Sir." Clegg threw the tablet aside.

Hodges made his way to the laboratory door. He opened it a crack and beckoned us forward. "All clear," he said.

And Operation Mother began.

We went through the levels, heading for the elevators that would take us straight to the Bulldog's "kennel." The men knew the way, which made me wonder how much of their knowledge was due to my minimal experience of this craft and how much might have come from Alexander's memories. *Had he been here like me?* I wondered. A boy immersed in a world of alien technologies and undercover activity? How much had he known — did the men now know? And what had gone so wrong between him and his father?

We moved through unhindered. No one paid me any more attention than they had when I'd done this with Agent Mulrooney. On the final escalator, we were joined by Dobbs and Grimper. They said nothing to Hodges and Clegg but just dropped into place on the step behind me.

At the top, we quickly progressed to the elevators. While Hodges and Clegg stood guard, Dobbs stopped me and whispered, "Goin' to need the override code now, sir." He nodded at the scanners, implying that men of their rank had no retinal pass to the Bulldog's level. I was in the system; the army wasn't. But what was the override code?

Two women stepped out of a neighboring elevator. They threw us a curious glance, clearly wondering why four anonymous men and a boy were hovering around, not going anywhere.

"Sir," Dobbs prompted. "Goin' to need those numbers."

And then I had an idea. In the factory, when I was pressing him for information, Alexander had given me his name and what sounded like his rank and serial number. But what if it was more than a serial number? What if he'd spoken a key? "41625 Dayton," I said.

Dobbs nodded. "41625. T D N A O. Got that?"

"Sarge," the others said. So he'd got the promotion he'd wanted after all.

"All right, lads, move it," said Dobbs. And while the others stepped into the adjoining elevators, he drew me into the nearest one with him.

The scanner immediately objected, not just to him but to what he was carrying. *Weapon detected*, it said. *Security breach in —*

"Special override," Dobbs cut in. "41625. T-D-N-A-O."

Lights went off in a panel in the roof. I held my breath, thinking we'd tripped an alarm or I'd simply been wrong about the code. But with a beep, the elevator confirmed the code and the door closed. "Level five," Dobbs said. We were on our way.

Safe inside the car, he produced the weapon from his uniform. Not the rifle he'd had on the Tommy cards but some kind of small, futuristic pistol — another gift of Alexander's mind, I guessed. He checked it, set a dial, and put it away.

For the first time, I began to have second thoughts. Thanks to me and a bunch of face-morphing soldiers, people could lose their lives here. "I want him alive," I said as strongly as I could.

Thankfully, Dobbs didn't argue. "Yes, sir. Fer the trial, sir."

Trial? What trial? What the heck had Alexander been planning?

"Don't worry. We'll make 'im talk," Dobbs said. He winked an eye slit and put a finger to his mouth. The elevator stopped and the doors swished open. Ahead of us was the corridor and the door to the Bulldog's office. Dobbs stepped out, keeping me behind him. He approached the door quietly with the gun hard-held.

"Where are the others?" I whispered.

"Hodges 'n' Clegg're on level four, sir, makin' sure we don't get interference. Grimps'll be at the other door now."

He checked a wristwatch and counted down with his fingers. 3 . . . 2 . . . 1.

And he burst into the office, crying, "Nobody move!" I heard a faint squeal of alarm. Then Grimper's voice joined in the shouting. "You! 'Ands on the desk where I can see 'em!"

Then Dobbs again. "Sir! All secure, sir! But target not found!"

What? I went in, shaking like crazy.

The men were posed in front of the desk, training their weapons on someone in the chair. I moved between them, confidently expecting to see Klimt with his hands held up in surrender.

But it wasn't the android. It was someone who should never have been there at all. A very small, very terrified little girl.

Josie.

"Michael?!" she squealed. "Who —?"

"I said don't move!" snapped Dobbs. A blue light from his pistol lit a spot on the center of Josie's forehead. A second spot from Grimper's gun danced alongside it.

"No!" I yelled at them. "This is my sister! She's not your enemy!"

"With respect, sir, could be a trap," said Grimper. He rested his pistol on his raised forearm.

"I said NO! Lower your weapons!"

They glanced at one another, their faces phasing into the army look. Josie saw the change and used both hands to stifle a scream.

"Dobbs, that's an order! Lower your gun!"

Backing down was not an option they were going to take lightly. I needed to show a stronger level of command or Josie and I were both in danger of being shot. "Guard the doors — while I interrogate the prisoner. Move!"

That did it. That was the tone they wanted. Dobbs

gestured with a flick of his head and they both fell back to cover the entrances.

Josie was bristling like a startled rabbit. "Wh-what *are* th-those . . . things?"

Stay calm, I mouthed. *I'll get you out. I promise.* "Shut up, girl. I ask the questions. Where's the Bulldog? Where's the old man?"

"I-I don't know who you mean," she stammered.

"She's lyin', sir," said Dobbs.

"Do your job, soldier! I'll deal with this. Who brought you here, girl?"

"Dr. K," she muttered. "Why are you being so horrible to me?" Her lower lip could not stop juddering.

"Klimt? The Bulldog's right-hand man?" Dobbs, I noticed, was taking this in.

She nodded again, her eyes darting between me and the men.

"Why? Why have they brought you here?"

Come on-nnn, Jose. She was delaying too long. I thumped the table. "Answer me, girl!"

"I was trying to call you," she squeaked, "but you weren't answering your phone. So I texted instead. And the next thing I knew, Dr. K and that nurse who looked after you when you had your accident came to the house."

"The French girl?"

"Yes. They had your phone."

My phone. I'd forgotten all about my phone. Chantelle must have found it on the factory floor after the fight with Alexander. It was still working then, despite being hurled at a wall? But they couldn't have been going to the house to return it, because they knew I was with Liam or in Preeve's lab. So they must have gone home to glamour Josie and bring her into the facility.

But why?

"Sir," Dobbs called. "Problem with the comms." He touched his ear. "I've lost contact with Hodges. Don't look good, sir. Smellin' a rat. Suggest we abort. Take the girl wiv us."

I winced and said, "I'm not done with her yet."

"Sir, Hodges and Clegg might be —"

"I said I'm not *done* here, soldier."

He dropped his shoulders. "Sir."

I looked at Josie and once again gestured for calm. I needed to think. But there was just no time. The only reason I had let this raid happen was to give the Bulldog some of his own medicine. It should have been him squirming in the chair. But with Josie in the room, my priorities had changed. Her safety was all that mattered to me now. There was no way I could disarm the men, so the only option was to stall until Klimt or his agents appeared. "You said text. What text?"

She started reaching into her jeans. Grimper saw the movement and shouted, "Hands on the table!"

Josie squealed as though she might wet herself.

"Hold your fire," I barked. "Let's see it, girl."

I nodded at Josie. *Show me.*

She bravely teased my mobile from her pocket, pushing it across the table like a plate of food she couldn't eat.

I opened my inbox and found her text.

Where r u? Called 2x when I got in frm drama. I worked out a bit of Dad's msg {{smug}}. He ♥ crosswrds. They have rules. I think 'New' means change the letters of MEXICO, like . . .

"COMIXE," I said, reading aloud the word she'd written.

She bit her lip. "It might be C O M I X with the *e* in front. Like eBook or even *e* colon *comix*."

Electronic comics. Wasn't that the prize Alexander had offered me? My story on a virtual platform? But how could that have a link to Dad? "What about the second part? 'Dragons abound'?"

She glanced at Grimper and shuddered. "Don't know."

"And Klimt brought you here because of this?"

"I don't *know*," she squeaked again. A tear wet her cheek. "I just . . . got here somehow, like I was dreaming. They said you were coming and I should just wait. They did this to me as well." She opened her top very slightly. To my horror, there was a single Mleptra on her chest. I'd never seen one outside the fluid tanks before. But it was definitely alive, radiating waves of color like fancy lights on a Christmas tree.

Before I could speak again, more lights began to flash in the ceiling panels. A grinding alarm went off. The two men quickly closed ranks, panning every quarter of the room with their weapons.

"Sir! Fall back, sir!" Dobbs yelled urgently, leveling his pistol at a panel to the right of Josie's head. It was opening slowly. At the same time, both the room doors slammed as if a seriously angry poltergeist were present. Grimper panicked and fired at his door, creating a crown of blue light and a smell of scorched wood at the point of contact. I glanced at Josie. Her hands were half-raised. She hadn't touched anything.

Grimper hurried to his door and rattled it. "Locked, Sarge! Can't move it!"

And all the while, the panel continued to open, revealing one of the tanks and its contents.

Dobbs stepped forward, taking closer aim. "What's that?" he shouted, which was why I didn't react as Josie did. I was looking for an object; she had seen a person.

She screamed so loudly I was sure the wall of the tank would crack.

Never, not even in my wildest reality shifts, had I expected to see what was in that tank. A semi-naked man, covered by so many glowing Mleptra that it looked as if they had replaced his skin and tattooed it every color of the rainbow. His eyes were closed, his wild brown hair streaming out into the fluid. Strands of Mleptral fibers were growing out of his fingers and toes, weaving around him in a sparkling web, as though he were encased in a cradle of wicker — or the branches of *The Tree of Life.*

"Sir, do you want me to shoot?" cried Dobbs.

I was too weak with shock to speak.

"Sir, do you *know* this target?"

"Yes," I managed to say at last. I leaned across the desk and gripped Josie's hand. "His name is Thomas Malone. He's my father."

Once, a couple of years ago, I had come downstairs after doing my homework and found Mom and Josie huddled up on the sofa, practically drowning in scrunched-up tissues. They were watching a TV documentary called *Long Lost Love*, one of those tearjerker programs where people are reunited with relatives they've lost contact with. I watched the presenter say, *Not only that, you thought your grandfather Bernard, was dead. But he isn't and we've found him. He's here tonight after thirty-two years* . . . Mom and Josie howled like a pair of wolves as this creaky old man was wheeled onto the set. I had made vomiting noises and Josie had hurled a cushion at my head and told me I had no soul. But no cushions were being thrown in the Bulldog's office. I looked at my father and started to shake uncontrollably. And though I cried no visible tears, I could feel myself dying from the inside out. It was him. No doubt about it. Thomas Stephen Malone. Missing, presumed dead, for three long years. Almost certainly here all the time. Not in New Mexico. Bound up instead by alien technology and some sort of failed experiment.

All of it clothed in Klimt's dark lies.

Dobbs shouted, "Grab the girl, sir! We'll cover yer."

"Drop your weapons," I muttered timidly. "The mission's over. Everything's over."

"Michael, I'm frightened." Josie was trembling, her throat almost wholly constricted by fear. Her eyes were like pools of shining mercury. So much pain in that one expression.

I leapt over the desk and got her out of the chair. "Drop your weapons," I barked again.

"Sir, request clarification!" yelled Dobbs. He took a shot at a beeping alarm. It kept on beeping.

I pressed Josie's head to my chest and said, "We can't win. We have to give up."

Dobbs looked at Grimper, who said, "Not an option, sir. We fight to the last. Them were yer primary orders."

Alexander's orders, maybe.

"We're trapped," I said, trying to reason with them. "Surrender and no one gets hurt."

There was a momentary pause. Dobbs checked his gun. "Is that a confirmation, sir? You want us to initiate surrender protocol?"

"Yes," I said.

His eye lines twitched. Both men were fully in the Tommy phase now. He nodded at Grimper, who briskly saluted.

"Been a pleasure servin' wiv you, sir," said Grimper.

And I thought he was going to lay down his arms, but as I took my eye off him to hug Josie tighter, I suddenly saw a blue light flickering in her hair.

When I looked up, Grimper had already fired. Light was streaming out of his pistol but hitting some kind of protective force field, shimmering violet around me and Josie. Dobbs also took aim and fired. The result was the same. More glowing violet. Only, this time, I noticed a small link back to the single Mleptra on Josie's chest. Somehow, the creature was absorbing the shots and at the same time shielding us from harm.

With a bang, the doors flew open. Chantelle and Mulrooney burst in. There was no battle, no exchange of fire. They simply shot the men before they could turn, using similar high-tech weapons. Dobbs exploded in front of my eyes, his body dissolving in a splash of mauve light as if he really was nothing more than a drawing. Just before he vanished, the ghostly shape of a Tommy soldier floated in the air where his head had been. It popped like a bubble — and he was gone.

The same fate befell Grimper, but with one important difference. Just before Chantelle zapped him, he had managed to pull a grenade from his jacket. It had barely left his hand when he was vaporized. Somehow, though, the grenade stayed live and tumbled under the Bulldog's desk.

"Get down!" I yelled, pulling Josie away.

Chantelle had seen it, but was too far back to do anything. I thought we were dead. Even with the Mleptran force field around us, the blast would surely rip a hole in the craft and we'd drown in a tide of cold seawater. But Mulrooney, still bruised from his brush with Alexander, had his own ideas about the grenade. Bravely, he put out his hand and used his power to draw it toward him. I could see what he was trying to do. If the grenade reached his hand in time, he could stop the mechanism and avoid a disaster.

But the seconds were ticking and I knew he wouldn't make it.

BANG! The grenade exploded in midair, just feet from his outstretched palm. He was lifted off the floor and thrown against the wall. Chantelle was carried sideways by the blast. Josie and I were rocked, but not harmed. Most importantly, the tank wasn't touched. In fact, nothing in the room suffered physical damage, but it was going to need a really good dustpan and brush to deal with the aftermath of the blast.

A strange winter had descended on the Bulldog's office.

The air was filled with paper streamers.

Josie gave a little gasp when she saw them. "*Hhh!* Are we in heaven?"

Only if angels let off party poppers when someone walks through the pearly gates. I touched her cheek and ran to Mulrooney. He was alive but hurt, struggling to stand.

"What happened? Where did all this come from?" He pulled a strand of crinkly paper from his hair.

"Another universe." I raised a guilty hand.

He high-fived it, despite his discomfort. "You are one weird Talen. You okay?"

"Could be better." I gestured at the tank.

He winced as his gaze drifted over it. "They showed you at last."

"How long have you known?"

He took a shuddering breath. "We were sworn to secrecy a long time ago. Thomas was my friend. I want you to know that."

I nodded but couldn't speak.

"The comic store," he said, gripping my arm. "The fire. Couldn't get to you in time. I'm sorry."

I nodded again. He had gold flecks everywhere. The complete ring of truth. He might have been UNICORNE through and through, but I'd always felt he was on my side.

Unlike Amadeus Klimt. I heard the sound of clapping over his voice. He was in the room, with the Bulldog right behind him. "Another fine display of your power, Michael, though as usual, you left it rather late."

"Get well," I said to Mulrooney. I patted his shoulder and picked up his gun.

"Michael, no!"

But he was too pained to stop me.

I ran back to Josie with the gun at arm's length. I grabbed her hand and moved her behind me. "One step closer and I'll melt your wires."

Wisely, Klimt stopped walking.

"Put the gun down," the Bulldog said gruffly.

"That includes you." I kept him in my sights as he walked to his chair.

He dusted the paper strips off his seat and sat down, throwing me a scornful look. "Your bravado is deeply misplaced. Thanks to you, I have lost a son, and UNICORNE has failed to recover a remarkable Talen. I'm not in the mood to be trifled with. Disarm him, please."

Something touched the back of my head. It felt horribly like the barrel of Chantelle's pistol.

"*Pour moi. Merci.*"

She pushed my head forward an inch.

I had no choice but to give up my gun.

"You leave him alone!" Josie said, storming forward, all her drama training coming to the fore. She banged her fists on the desk and squared up to the Bulldog. "Who are you? Why have you brought us here? What have you done to my dad?" Before he could answer, she had turned on Klimt. "And *you're* not even a proper doctor!"

"Klimt, get her out," the Bulldog said.

Klimt nodded at Chantelle.

"Hey, Josie?" she said.

"What?!" Josie whipped around and gave Chantelle the full-on, ten-year-old, don't-mess-with-me STARE.

"Why don't we go and get ice cream?"

In the circumstances, this seemed a bizarre thing to say. But as soon as Josie muttered, "Can we have strawberry?" I knew it was a pre-prepared glamouring suggestion.

"*Mon préféré,*" said Chantelle. "Oh, allow me." She parted Josie's top just enough to be able to remove the Mleptra.

Josie reached out and stroked it. "What is it?"

"A source of wonder," Chantelle said. And she took Josie's hand and led her out, handing the creature to Klimt as she passed. I wasn't happy about letting them take her, but deep down, I was sure she wouldn't be harmed. It was one less complication to have her out of the way.

Mulrooney was on his feet by now, winded and clutching his ribs. He hobbled over to Klimt and exchanged a few words. To my horror, I watched Klimt crush the Mleptra and let the juice fall into Mulrooney's hand. It was blue, like the stuff I'd seen Klimt drink. Mulrooney swallowed what he could of it. He grimaced, but immediately stood more erect. He nodded at me and walked out of the room as if he'd suffered nothing but a minor bump.

Shaken, I went and stood by the tank, with my father floating eerily beside me. Staying as calm as I could, I said, "I'm learning to control my reality shifts. Next time I do it, neither of you will exist in this universe if you don't tell me everything I want to know."

The Bulldog took an impatient breath. He rocked in his chair and gave me a never-work-with-children-or-animals look.

"WELL?" I roared.

Klimt took a handkerchief from his pocket and wiped his hands clean of the alien tissue. He hitched up a trouser leg and perched himself on a corner of the desk. "Once again, we need to talk about your loyalty, Michael. Twice you have severely disappointed us. You knew what had happened to Alexander's men, yet you led them against us. Why?"

"Why do you think?" I waved toward the tank. "How long has he *been* like this?"

"His body was placed in the care of the Mleptra shortly after he returned from New Mexico."

"He never *went* to New Mexico."

"And what makes you say that?"

"The message he left for Liam Nolan. The code that Josie cracked. What does *COMIXE* mean?"

"It means nothing," he said, brushing a speck of dust off his trousers. "The message was meaningless — though I agree, your sister has a powerful intellect. She might even be of use to us one day." I started with the threats again, but he raised his voice and spoke right over me. "Do not concern yourself about Josie. She will leave here remembering nothing. It is a pity you allowed her to become involved. We had no choice but to bring her in once we read her . . . creative text. Fortunately, she spoke of it to no one but you." He raised a finger to cut me off again. "The only reason we put her in the room was to calm you down and bring you to your senses. We suspected you were preparing an attack when the override code was put into the elevator. Your attempted coup was deeply misguided. You are lucky to be alive."

"You're lying. That message *has* to mean something. It was hidden in an envelope in Dad's old study."

"Located behind *The Tree of Life* painting, which Freya successfully guided you to."

I switched my gaze between them. "How did you know?"

"Because we planted it there," said the Bulldog.

"You must improve your security," said Klimt. "It was a simple matter for Agent Mulrooney to break into your home when the house was empty and place the envelope behind the print. And before you ask, yes, it was your father's hand-writing. We have many samples — and Chantelle is very skilled in the art of forgery. After that, it was simply a case of imprinting the image of *The Tree of Life* in Freya's mind. She led you to it and you did the rest."

"You mean, you *wanted* me to take the message to Nolan? Why?"

Klimt folded his arms, dusting an arc of the floor with his shoe. "Well, there we have our dilemma. Do we trust you with this information or not?"

I reached sideways and touched the wall of the tank, watching the Mleptral fibers pulse.

The Bulldog said, "I let you see your father as a gesture of faith. A final gesture, Michael. Klimt, show him the photograph."

Klimt pulled a tablet computer from his jacket. He showed me a picture of Liam Nolan with a woman.

"Is that —?"

"Candy Streetham, yes. The journalist who was keen to investigate your previous mission. Chantelle has been tracing her movements. It would seem that Ms. Streetham has started to research your father's disappearance. We are concerned that Dr. Nolan might be passing information to her. We set you up with the message to test his reaction, knowing that you would . . . inflame the situation. He knows we believe that Thomas is alive. Despite being your father's doctor and confidant, he might be suffering a crisis of conscience and wanting to speak about what he knows, or thinks he knows. That is something we cannot tolerate."

"Has he seen the tank?"

"No."

"And has he spoken to Candy since . . . ?"

"No," Klimt said, "but we are watching him, of course. His loyalty, for now, is still intact. He did, after all, restrain you when ordered."

Hmph. The less said about that, the better. "Will you tell me what happened with Dad? How did he end up like this, covered by hundreds of alien creatures?" One of them lifted off Dad's shin and reattached itself to the corresponding hip. "What planet are these things from?"

"This planet," the Bulldog said.

I laughed. "You expect me to believe that?"

The Bulldog sighed. "Klimt, this is —"

"The first time we met," I said angrily, over him, "you were wearing contact lenses with gold-colored specks to make me think you were telling the truth." I gave him a knowing look.

He sat back slowly, blowing air down his nose like a weary horse. He smiled at me, knowing I'd scored a point.

"The director is speaking the truth," Klimt said. "The beings were found on an artifact your father brought back from New Mexico. They were microscopic then, engaged in what is known as a symbiotic relationship with their host. They grew in culture until they reached the size you see here. They are a hivelike organism with extraordinary healing properties. We still have much to learn about them."

"You crushed one. Why?"

"It was a cell, Michael. One small cog in a very big wheel. Mulrooney's need was greater than the hive's. The energy required to protect you and Josie had also weakened it. It was almost dead. Terminating it carried no real consequence."

"Is that what they're doing? Healing Dad? What's wrong with him? Why is he in the tank?"

Klimt pushed himself away from the desk. He came to stand beside me, facing the tank. As he peered through the membranous wall, I thought I saw sorrow in his eyes again. Was it possible Dad had installed some kind of emotional coding in the android? Something that made him at least *partially* human? Lacing his perfect fingers, he said, "He complained of dizziness on the mission. A fever. Unexpected hallucinations. We brought him home in a private aircraft that the civil authorities could not trace. This, of course, was one of the details that first gave rise to the idea he was missing."

"Why a private aircraft?"

"The Mleptra would not have been allowed on a commercial flight. And we could not risk further . . . contamination."

"Contamination? But I thought they were . . . friendly?"

Now it was his turn to smile. "Director, do I have your permission to take Michael to the artifact room?"

The Bulldog rumbled like his namesake animal and pinched a flap of loose skin under his chin. "How badly do you want your father back, boy?"

"I'd do anything. You know I would."

"Anything? Even risk your own life? How do you think your mother would cope with that?"

"She'd be proud of me."

"No, boy, she wouldn't. She'd hate you for potentially doubling her loss. Just like Alexander's mother resented me for making him a part of UNICORNE. He was one of our best. Our very best. So good that I allowed him to experience the DNA program. You saw what it did. It enhanced his powers and drove him insane. It made him commit a terrible act. One day, when you've hardened your queasy little stomach, I'll let Klimt give you all the details. Even then, I'd lay a dollar you'll lose your lunch. So when I ask if you're willing to risk your life, consider what you've seen these past few days, *then* give your answer." He leaned forward, hardening his gaze. "Any more threats or petulant mistakes and you'll wake up one morning with a head full of cotton candy. Do I make myself clear?"

If I haven't buried you first, I thought.

"I need to hear you say it, Michael."

"Yes," I said, biting my tongue.

He paused for a moment and swung his chair. "What Klimt will show you is highly classified. As is this." He unlocked a drawer and dropped a folder marked THOMAS MALONE on his desk. "Bedtime reading. Strictly under the covers. Klimt, take him to the artifact room. Then begin his preparation."

"Preparation?" I said. "For what?"

"Your brush with dragons," he said.

And he nodded at the door to say we were done — as if it was the last time he would ever see me.

ACKNOWLEDGMENTS

As always, I'd like to extend my thanks to everyone involved in the production of this book, both home and abroad. It doesn't matter how many times you're published, the thrill remains the same, and you can't achieve anything without a dedicated team. But two people do deserve particular mention. First, Lisa Sandell, who fought my corner at what could have been a difficult moment. And also Jay d'Lacey, who gave me the initial idea of the army. Read it with the lights on. Enjoy.

CHRIS D'LACEY

is the author of several highly acclaimed books, including the *New York Times* bestselling Last Dragon Chronicles: *The Fire Within, Icefire, Fire Star, The Fire Eternal, Dark Fire, Fire World,* and *The Fire Ascending.* Additionally, he is the author of the middle grade series The Dragons of Wayward Crescent. He lives in Devon, England, with his wife, where he is at work on his next book. You can visit Chris online at www.theunicornefiles.wordpress.com.

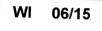